(Ex Libris)

Dedicated to free Amerika

Adolph Menzel

THE DAYS OF THE KING

A Novel by Bruno Frank

TRANSLATED BY H. T. LOWE-PORTER

WITH A FOREWORD BY SINCLAIR LEWIS

AND ILLUSTRATIONS BY ADOLF VON MENZEL

The Press of THE READERS CLUB

NEW YORK

FOREWORD

"COPYRIGHT 1924 by Ernst Rowohlt in Berlin."
That is the melancholy notice in the first
American edition of this book; sad in its mem-
ory of the frustration of a great world promise.
In 1924, Ernst was the jolliest and most hope-

ful of publishers, young, round, laughing, fonder of nothing more than of a drink at the Adlon bar with the American and English authors whom he was proud of introducing to a New Germany that was surely cured forever of the St. Vitus Dance of war. In no city, ever, had the cafés been more shining than in Berlin then, nor the dancing more lively and innocent-seeming, nor the *apéritif*-talk more friendly and international.

An intimate of Ernst was Bruno Frank, a statelier man, but as solemnly fond of practical jokes on the unweaned American tourist: a man of the most polished brilliance — scholar, novelist, dramatist, author of the play *Twelve Thousand,* which portrayed the Hessians who were to be sold into service against the American Revolution. Everything about Bruno Frank was highlighted. His wife was and is the lovely Liesl, who was the step-daughter of Max Pallenberg, greatest of mid-European comedians — *der liebe Max,* who was later killed in an aeroplane, on his way to an engagement at Salzburg — and the daughter of the radiant

vi

Fritzi Massary, the most beautiful, the most melodious operetta star of Germany and Austria.

When Hitler first became perceptible, as a symptomatic itch, Bruno and Liesl came to America, not in the panic flight which was afterward to devastate many of their colleagues but with a perception, remarkable even in so sound an historian as Bruno Frank, that Germany was no longer to be a home for free and honest men.

He lives now, with Liesl, with Mme. Fritzi close at hand, near the Pacific, in Los Angeles. Among his neighbors — now, in late 1941, with the Japs snooping about, the Japs who would hate a man like Bruno Frank — are Thomas Mann and Franz Werfel and Lion Feuchtwanger and Lewis Browne and Theodore Dreiser and Leopold Stokowski and James Hilton and Aldous Huxley and Arnold Schönberg.

We forget that the name of Los Angeles means that it is the city of the angels, not the city of realtors and press-agents and cosmetics. With such approximations to angelhood as

vii

Bruno Frank, sent to us by the extreme thoughtfulness of Adolf Hitler, and with its Mediterranean sky and hills, Los Angeles may really be on its way to becoming the new Florence that its advertising men think it already is. Such streamlined prophets can sometimes (by accident) be right!

Bruno Frank has been in America long enough now, and contentedly enough, so that we may now claim him, and have a more nearly native interest in THE DAYS OF THE KING than when it was first published here, in 1927. It is more important now, in any case.

Since it was first published, biography and the biographical novel have become bolder, more human: and here is a biographical novel bold and brave and particularly human.

Its importance lies in its lucid glimpse of that most astounding of all human freaks, a genuine Great Man.

A clever man, a mere capable man, is less than the sum of all his parts. He doesn't quite achieve what you would expect from, say, his skill in languages *plus* his handsome nose *plus*

viii

his kindness to his mother *plus* his technique of love-making. But a true Great Man is recognized by the fact that he miraculously adds up to more than all his various parts put together.

Frederick the Great, who is the center of THE DAYS OF THE KING, was a drillmaster rather than a strategist—yet he was a great general; he was an intriguer rather than a diplomat—yet he was a great statesman; he was a sentimentalist who fawned on dogs, and a *diletiante* who composed for the flute; he was an exhibitionist who hated people too much to endure having them about to exhibit to; he was a twisted and violent misanthrope who could yet be loved by such opposites as Voltaire and Lafayette. And all these eccentricities, chemically combined, came out as positive Greatness.

In this story, Bruno Frank makes the character, Henschke, perceive it, as he looks at the sleeping monarch:

"What he had before him was heroism, the height of the human spirit; here it lay, encased in that pitiable little frame, that perishable, unpretentious husk. He [Henschke] said to himself: 'This is the climax of my life, my great moment . . . This old, ailing man, the King of kings, the first among men, he lies here before me.' "

In three swift incidents, Bruno Frank gives us more of the essence of Frederick's greatness — and his loneliness — than would a library of dates and battle-maps. Here is the ruler, in one cold corner of his palace, alone with an aged friend; then, drilling his cavalry so arduously that he is more of a pain than a glory in the noble eyes of such military observers as Lord Cornwallis (late of Brooklyn, U.S.A.); then, over the death of his little exquisite Italian greyhound, he is shedding the tears which are the last relief he is likely ever to know.

The real man is in the chronicle, and the reader will not so much know a lot about this grey and black magician, Frederick, as know the man himself.

SINCLAIR LEWIS

X

A NOTE

UPON THE ILLUSTRATIONS

FREDERICK THE SECOND, King of Prussia, was an enlightened leader of men; a magnificent soldier; a poet; and an intimate, as well as a patron, of Voltaire and the other great minds of his time. Around him there has grown a towering monument of books, including biographies by Thomas Carlyle and Thomas Macaulay. Among these, perhaps the greatest is Franz Kugler's *History of Frederick the*

Great. Another, equally monumental, work is Frederick's own collected writings in thirty-one volumes, *The Works of Frederick the Great.* Yet, of the thousands of *documents* which aid in our understanding of Frederick, none is more valuable than the wood-engravings of Adolf Menzel!

Adolf Friedrich Erdmann von Menzel was born in 1815, and died in 1905. He was famous as a painter; dozens of his important canvases hang in the important galleries of the world. But he devoted many years to the illustration of Frederick the Great's *Memoirs* and Kugler's *History.* He made hundreds of illustrations, which were engraved in wood. He translated Frederick into a man people could understand: by depicting the Great Man in solemnity and in smiles, in high good humor and in wrath; by depicting Frederick's homes, his friends, his dogs, his clothes, his hand while writing.

With the engraving of these hundreds of illustrations, Adolf Menzel gave a new impetus to the art of book illustration. Whenever col-

xii

lectors of illustrated books discuss the few great illustrated books of all time, they include the engravings made by Adolf Menzel for *The Works of Frederick the Great.* This is commonly considered the triumph of book illustration in Germany in the nineteenth century. For achieving it, Menzel was awarded the Order of the Black Eagle in 1898, which confers upon its holder the privilege of hereditary nobility. One must remember that, in 1898, Hitler was not yet an odor in the nostrils of the peoples of the world; he was only the odoriferous young Adolf Schickelgruber then, and people could still see the nobility in the German character.

So The Readers Club has obtained a complete set of prints of Menzel's wood-engravings, prints made directly from the engravings themselves, which are now in the National Gallery in Berlin. The editors have gone through the prints, and selected seven dozen of these remarkable illustrations for reproduction in this edition of Bruno Frank's novel THE DAYS OF THE KING.

CONTENTS

AUTHOR'S PREFACE

GREAT HEROES *have this in common with great poets, that both address the general ear of mankind. Our poor efforts appeal to this audience, or that: perhaps to youth, perhaps to wise old age, perhaps to women, or tired and busy men, or elegant amateurs. But in great poetry everyone finds his own; it is a tree that gathers all the world beneath its shade. And so with the great dead. Frederick's fearlessness, his stern-*

ness with himself, his unswerving purpose, are stuff to strengthen youth. His gift of combining enormous industry with the gratification of his intellectual tastes is a sermon for riper years. His bare integrity, magnificent resignation, and frightful clarity of vision all grip the mind of age. In him the elements of intellect, of moral strength and sheer humanity were so combined as to make him an indispensable model to any people—his own today the most of all.

And yet: to turn the name of this preternaturally—well-nigh inexplicably—rich and gifted being into a chauvinistic rallying-cry is about as profound, and about as justifiable, as to reduce the whole of Tristan *and* Isolde *to a formula, and say: "Well, after all, love is a wonderful thing."*

When Frederick died, there followed his little corpse a perfect cataract of literature: descriptive, rhapsodic, and even abusive. But while he still lived he had become a legend and a theme. His people saw this world-renowned old man, shrunken and sickly, in a shabby coat, almost incorporeal, go posting and peering, in dust and heat, up and down his lands; and no travesty of his actions was too strong, no situation too fantastic, for them to credit him with it.

We approach him today in a less venturesome mood: we merely recall. For these torchlit carriages did drive in protest beneath his windows; this fateful scar he actually concealed upon his body; and over an exquisite little corpse taken out of the grave he did in very truth shed these tears.

The Lord Chancellor

H E had come alone from Potsdam to the city, expressly to make an end of the Arnold affair; and sat now in the poorest room of this castle that he did not like: a one-windowed, narrow closet, scantily furnished and heated to suffocation by a primitive stove hastily set up. He was dressed as always, carelessly and meanly as never the lowest quartermaster in a West-Prussian garrison: with shabby riding-breeches and clumsy boots he wore a blue velvet top-coat turning green at the seams, and on his head, an extraordinary

habit of his since the Ahasuerus-years of the great campaign, a battered old military hat mounted askew, the general's plume torn off and threads hanging down from the place. Curled he was not, scarcely properly washed; the hair on one side of his head was already white, on the other greyish, in his mouth still stuck a few yellow stumps of teeth, the body was warped by gout and made no pretensions to carriage. The King was an unkempt, unlovely sight. But the eyes, the great, strange-shaped eyes, in which the white almost always showed above the iris — they gleamed triumphant over this ruin, like the sun above a standing pool.

In such a guise had no other king gone about in his rooms — never in this formal and pomp-loving century, and perhaps in none. Of that he was aware. Even though one be the heart and brain of his state, even though one drudge fourteen hours in the day, even then one can find time to dress, and give one's person a little care — if only one has the mind. But this, out of sheer contempt, he had not. Out of contempt for the rococo type of royalty that spent its days dressing and dining; out of contempt for his ministers, generals, and functionaries, in their gala array; out of contempt for his body, which would not endure, which was stooping toward the grave; out of contempt for the grave, and wanting to leave nothing for it to take away; out of contempt for life itself, which seemed to him so brief and lamentable a matter, so bare of every hope that he could not

5

bring himself to honour it even by a hygienic practice or so. But still another and quite special reason there was, why he let himself so degenerate and fall away, and felt a secret joy at the wretched figure he cut. He weighed his deeds, he saw his states, he knew his fame, that sped winged across seas and mountains. He knew he was spoken of with bated breath, whispered of in the tongues of white and yellow and brown men; he knew his legendary portrait hung in the houses of great and small, the cynosure of all eyes; and it gave him a bad and bitter joy to distort and mutilate the original of that legend. Yes, he was pleased when he lost a tooth, pleased that his clothing reeked with the sour, fusty smell of stale tobacco. It was fine to sit here so poor, so sunk, in this brooding warmth, in a sort of linen-room, and know that the whole race of living men exalted him to the skies, that he would shine there like a constellation, unchangeable throughout the ages. It was something very high, very fine, which he sat there cynically savouring: a genuine, a fundamental triumph of mind over matter.

6

He sat crouched in the arm-chair. One hand, that ached almost unbearably, he had stuck in the large shabby muff beside him on a table. At his other hand was another such table, holding an agate box overloaded with brilliants, from which he kept taking snuff; and beside the box a pile of documents. One of these he held in his free and sounder hand. It commenced with the words: "In the Name of the King," and it was a legal instrument. He knew, who knew every-

7

thing about his kingdom, that the formula was the regular and prescribed one. But it pleased him to forget that fact. He wanted to regard the invocation of his authority as a particular, a unique encroachment; wanted to, and did.

"A cruel abuse of my name!" he said aloud, and the veins on his grey old temples swelled. "But just wait, *canaille!*"

It was a small civil case. The Count of Schmettau, a Frankfort magnate, was about to sell up a certain miller, lessee of a water-mill, for not paying his rent. The miller protests he is not at fault: the District President of Gersdorff, a relative of Schmettau, has built a fishpond on the brook above the mill, which draws off the water and impoverishes him. The Cüstrin court decides against the miller. The miller appeals to the King. The King invokes his *Kammergericht,* invokes his Lord High Chancellor, the highest luminary of civil jurisprudence in the kingdom. The case goes against the miller. The mill will be sold at auction. There can be no further appeal, all legal resources have been exhausted.

For months the King has been obsessed by this affair. When in the winter nights his gout lets him fall asleep, he starts up in a fever of the spirit. His sense of justice has been wounded and is hot. The great man cannot be right against the small — it is a maxim of the other world, and void of all logic and thereby the more unimpeachable. Ah, why must a man's powers be hampered? Why were there laws and officials for the conduct of a state, why was he not enough, he single-handed? The King, he had said, is the first servant of his realm; but his wish, his tormenting dream it was to be not the first but the only one. He mistrusted everybody; in his deep knowledge of the frailty of the human heart, he ascribed to himself alone the will to be upright, to help and to heal. He would have liked to try, and to decide, every cause in his kingdom: the quarrels of provinces among themselves, of communities, of families, of blood-brothers. In the human beings he ruled over he saw a poor stock indeed, but even more a pitiful and an afflicted one. He longed for a giant's fabulous strength that he might do everything himself. For the occupants of other thrones, who went in fine array, kept women and gave fêtes, he felt unutterable disgust; what he would have liked was to carry in his arms the habitable globe — this no longer out of the smallest lust of power, for he was sated with wars and conquests; no, but out of a lust of service. At Heaven he spat, declared it was empty air; yet liked to scoff at the conception of a ruler sitting enthroned and so lamentably exercising his regal functions, letting so much misery and wrong hold sway in the planet he was supposed to govern.

But here, here — the palsied hand shook and crumpled the paper he held — here he had ferreted out a pattern of the universal baseness and injustice, and he pounced on it like a gift from heaven. Ah, in Prussia at least, he was on guard, he was king enough and man enough to throttle presumption in high and official places! He did not trouble to read the grounds on which the decision rested, there could be none. He fixed upon the formula "In the Name of the King," and the blood of a hidebound and

outraged parent throbbed in his old temples almost to bursting.

The clock struck five, in clear, brisk tones, and on the stroke the Heyduck entered and announced the judges. With his right and sounder foot the King knocked over the little green-upholstered bench in front of him. Let them in! He was as angry as heart could wish.

There entered the Lord Chancellor Freiherr von Fürst, Rebeur, President of the *Kammergericht,* and the two counsellors. He, instead of greeting them, drew his grotesque hat lower on his brow, and measured the men who halted before him in a little row. At length he spoke, crumpling the document in his hand:

"So," he said, "it is you who have done this?"

The three judges bowed, and murmured something. The Chancellor, a distinguished figure in full court dress, went a patchy red and clenched his teeth.

"It's a shabby piece of business—and a shameful."

The Lord Chancellor could contain himself no longer. "If Your Majesty will pardon me—"

12

"I will pardon you nothing. You confirmed the decision, I know it for a fact, you'll not fool me."

The Lord Chancellor looked him forbiddingly in the face. He came of a great house, was very affluent, very travelled, inured to every social success; proud, and not without reason, of his blameless conduct of his office; supremely scornful of this trumpery affair he

13

was involved in; and unshakable in the conviction that he had thoroughly investigated the case and rendered a just decision. With a sort of gloomy disgust he eyed the god-forsaken, stubborn old man, who looked, sitting there in the arm-chair, a proletarian caricature of his own world-wide renown.

"You there," Frederick said, and turned to Graun, Counsellor to the *Kammergericht,* a little fat man in an embroidered uniform, who looked lowest in rank of the four. "Answer me, you: what did Schmettau pay you for the verdict?"

This was his fixed idea. He believed every official, every judge, to be venal; and declared that he gave such poor salaries simply on the ground that the *canaille* knew so well how to piece out their pay.

"Paid?" the fat man stammered. "The Count of Schmettau paid us nothing."

"Surely Your Majesty does not think," said President Rebeur, a well-preserved old man with a clear, friendly eye, "that a Prussian court renders judgment except in accordance with its conscience?"

14

The King squinted at him and muttered an objurgation.

"The miller asserts that the carp-pond draws off the water from his mill. But between the pond and the Arnold mill there is another mill, a saw-mill—"

"Another mill, saw-mill," screamed the King. "So you think you can gull me, do you? You won't put me off the scent!" He screamed because he felt a practical objection coming, and wanted to hear none of it.

But the President was not to be diverted from his train of thought. "This saw-mill, Your Majesty, could not function either, if the miller were right. But it functions capitally; so the miller must be wrong and the Count von Schmettau right. This is the ground the Cüstriner verdict rests upon, and ours as well," he concluded, motioning with his head toward the crumpled roll the King still held in his hands.

Frederick got up. He erected himself on his cane, gave a short groan and turned it into a cough. Then he began to stump up and down the room, limping. The three judges followed him with their eyes; the Lord Chancellor

15

scorned to do so, and stared frigidly straight
ahead.

Frederick's imagination worked better when
he was on his legs; he had got up with the in-

stinctive design to stimulate it. He had the
greater need of strong emotions and vivid pictures, for the facts the President had brought
forward seemed incontrovertible in logic. He
gathered all his powers to project his fancy and
visualize the miller's plight.

16

He saw the royal servants of justice enter the peasant room, with their three-cornered hats and black portfolios; saw them place the royal seal, with the royal coat of arms, on the humble household effects; saw in a corner the wailing wife, and the unconscious children whose patrimony was being taken from them. The miller was there, silent, helpless; his thick head filled with the one idea, that now the appeal to the King had borne no fruit, that the King himself was powerless against the oppression of the great, that even in Prussia the poor are only the poor, without rights, wretched. Now the man went forth from the house that was no longer his. He gave one more glance at the brook, gliding so shallow and sluggishly that the *Landrat* might fatten his carp and the *Landrat's* cousin sell up the mill. He stood with his family on the high-road, roofless, breadless, a subject unjustly punished, and rebellious; neither did he know where to turn, or whether to take the left-hand road into the Obrabruch or the right-hand one to Schwiebus; dully indifferent which, since now in Prussia

17

no justice could be found . . . not even in the King.

Ah, now he had his feelings where he wanted them! He stepped close before the judges, he hissed up at them:

"You shan't make a fool of me! None of that rigmarole of yours puts me off. You shall pay me for Arnold's property with your own — and the rest we shall soon see."

The Lord Chancellor stepped a pace back from the furious old man. "Your Majesty," he began, firmly.

"Hold your tongue!" shrieked Frederick.

It was the last straw. That piece of frigid elegance there only had to rub him the wrong way! He was glad through and through. He welcomed the chance to send this aristocrat packing with a sting in his tail. For he had a reason, a serious and weighty reason, quite and entirely apart from the Arnold affair.

"I must request my discharge from the service of Your Majesty's government."

"Request, hey? You request? Get along with you, then, get out!"

18

The Lord Chancellor stood pale as a corpse, trying to pull himself together.

"Marche, marche," screamed the King, falsetto. "Your successor has been appointed." And with the thick end of his cane he struck the door so violent a blow that it shook from top to bottom.

The Lord Chancellor looked hard at the King, then without bowing turned and left.

"Cruelly misused my name — and then brazen into the bargain!" the King bawled after him. He railed like a shrew. His eyes glittered, he revelled in the thoroughly unkingly scene he was enacting.

"Well, and the rest of you," he said to the others, standing there stock-still. "What are you waiting for? Pack yourselves off, wait for your sentence!"

But when they had gone out and traversed the length of three rooms, they heard him come up behind them, crying out: "Wait, wait!"

They stood still again, dazed, resigned. Presently an officer appeared; he had orders to convey them to the public prison. He was abashed and obsequious, he knew he had before him the foremost judges in the kingdom. With embarrassed face he led the three gentlemen down the steps. From his narrow window up above, the King watched them mount into the coach.

Twilight had fallen when he turned back into the room. He fetched a taper, lit it, set it on one of the little tables, sat painfully down again, and fumbled among his papers. He took in his hand a communication from von Zedlitz, Minister of Justice, head of the Criminal Department. The King had lately commissioned him to sentence the counsellors of the *Kammergericht* to prison. Zedlitz wrote:

"I have had the favour of Your Royal Majesty ever in my eye as the greatest happiness of my whole life, and I have zealously laboured to be worthy of it. But I should count myself unworthy indeed, were I to embark on a line of conduct contrary to my convictions."

Frederick's face as he read was not angry, but neither did it express any of the esteem which was the upright and honest man's just due. His eyes, half sad, half mocking, betrayed both pity and contempt for this stiff-necked human pride in the face of thrones. He laid hold of his pen, and bending laboriously forward with the portfolio on his knees, he scribbled the following:

"The gentleman's remarks do not take me in. I am acquainted with lawyers' tricks and decline to be bamboozled. A justice who is guilty of chicanery must be punished with greater severity than a highway robber. For you have trusted the first, while you are on your guard against the second."

He folded this ready for the seal and tossed it down. But then he drew a long breath, he sat up straight, a smile visited his face, a different, quite spontaneous and genuine smile. Carefully he chose a fresh sheet of paper, and examined it on both sides to make sure it was clean. Then he slowly dipped the pen in the ink, and wrote the superscription in clear, round characters: "My dear Lord Chancellor von Carmer." It was the commission of the new appointee.

But for the present he left it at that. He prolonged the instant of fulfilment, he lingered it out, he savoured a moment of profound, transcendent pleasure, that repaid him for all his pains and fatigues, his sufferings and isolation.

"My dear Lord Chancellor von Carmer!"

Frederick's moments of actual triumph were not always the ones blazoned to the world. Sixteen years before, when he returned from his war against Europe, his people had looked up to him, and thought to share his greatest hour. The city of Berlin had sent a gala coach to the gates, drawn by horses in gilded trappings. But he could not bring himself to enter it. In his own travelling-coach he took his way by side streets to the castle. This war, this triumph, this peace lay æons behind him, they were no longer a cause for jubilation. He did not hang upon outward signs, he lived and thought in centuries.

And his stolen moment of triumph, here in this little room—it too had to do with a work that should endure through centuries.

The law of the land! His goal and preoccupation for more than a generation; attacked by him as a young monarch, with Cocceji's aid: the great codification, the comprehensive civil code of a justice that should be after his own heart and mind, a swift, durable justice, founded on reason, right, and equity, to the abiding security of state and subjects. But then had come the wars, and after them interminable work, pressing, importunate, tangible tasks, that filled each day brim-full; there had been the bloodless acquisition of new provinces, and peaceful penetration of those acquired by the sword. Cocceji dead, the plan he

had drawn up had been forgotten, even the manuscript of it was lost. Only seldom and shamefacedly did the King still mention the great project, only now and then did he express his feeling that justice was beginning again to slumber.

All too deep, even so, her slumber could not be, with him at hand to rouse her! But one day soon he too would be lying in his last sleep, and then who would be on guard? The thought of death, these last years, left him no moment's peace—his body, indeed, was lavish with warning signs. Must he leave behind him a state in which the old, bad, unclear laws were still on the books, a state where without his imminent eye the administration of justice would soon slip back into chaos and procrastination? He needed a buttress, he needed a foundation, he had no right to lie down in death before at least the cornerstone was laid fair.

And then, five years ago now, Carmer had appeared. It was in Neisse, the evening after a grand review. He had sought an audience as the first administrator of Silesia; and he en-

tered Frederick's presence with more self-assurance, more freedom from restraint, than the
King's officials were wont to have, a Rhine-
lander by birth, with an urbanity of manner
almost French. He asked leave to develop his
project. It would take two hours, perhaps
more.

Frederick nodded. He was tired from long
riding, from sun and dust, but he listened; at
first with an effort, then suddenly broad awake

and genuinely enthusiastic. Yes, this was his way, this his plan.

The common law! Not a mere collection of civil precedents, but a comprehensive code which should create stable and universal conceptions where before had been vacillation and room for arbitrary action. Tenets of political science should be in it, norms for social legislation, sections of criminal law, legal procedure. It almost frightened the King, to hear how precise was Carmer's knowledge of all the gaps and defects in the present system. If revolutionists were to be cut from such timber the throne would totter.

There must be abridgment of legal procedure; dilatory trials served the propertied classes against the poor, whose means, of course, were sooner exhausted. Oral proceedings then, interrogation by the judge instead of the interminable taking of written evidence. Simplification of the stages of appeal. Protection of the peasant class against the nobility. But also protection of the landed property of the nobility against the encroachments of

26

bourgeois capital. War on industrial depression; safe-guarding the right to work. Protection of labour in growing industries. Safeguards against the exploitation of depression in wages; prevention of arbitrary dismissal. Guarantee of freedom of conscience, definition of the rights of State and Church.

And then the mighty marshalling of single laws. The King, quite contrary to his habit, scarcely interrupted. Only when Carmer discussed the criminal law did he indicate a few reforms that lay near his heart: demanded a

27

milder punishment for infanticide, for theft due to destitution. Then Carmer held on with his exposition, free without notes, forcible, convincing.

It was late in the night when Frederick dismissed the jurist. His mind was made up. This was his code. This was his man. But it would

28

hardly answer to call Carmer to Berlin without more ado. Chancellor von Fürst's conduct of his office gave no opening, and he had done good service in his time as special envoy to Vienna, and after that in Western Prussia. Frederick sought to associate the two men; it proved impossible. Carmer was a thinker and originator, Fürst a bureaucrat, conservative to the backbone, with an obstinate sense of dignity, unfriendly to compromise. Ten times the King was at the point of brusquely effecting the change, ten times he shrank from deposing the blameless man from office. But he waited for the hour to strike. He must get himself a justification for doing the Chancellor this wrong — a wrong which in a higher sense was a right. In the meantime Carmer, at his post in Silesia, in the quiet of his office worked on his task. Was it just to keep him waiting on in uncertainty? Men are mortal. Mortal above all was the King himself. And it was his nightly dread, this thought that he must leave his kingdom unsecured, leave it in the hands of a lax and limited successor. Fürst must go. His

tall, elegant figure barred the way to a door
that must be forced open. Well, today, at last,
the passage had been forced, the door stood
open. "My dear Lord Chancellor von Carmer!"

Moment of happiness, moment of consum-
mation. With his eyelids closed the King
leaned back in his chair. His hand did not pain
him, it was perfectly still in the room, the taper
flared and its yellow light danced. He had
reached his goal, he might be utterly frank
with himself. Yes: he had taken up the cudgels
for a subject, flung himself with passion into
the feelings of a lowly lot; he had let compas-
sion swell within his breast, and outrage
against overbearing power. He had hunted
this lawsuit through all its appeals, had swept
away every pretext by a peremptory decision,
had practised Star-Chamber methods which
otherwise he held taboo — and he had done all
this quite sincerely, yet with an ulterior mo-
tive; his decision had been freely made, yet
made in the consciousness of an overruling des-
tiny; he had not been supported, nor sanc-

tioned, he had made it wholly alone, he was responsible only to himself. His smile grew harder, it passed over into a grin. No, it would scarcely have been quite easy to make clear, to his Brother of France, for instance, the paths in which he, Frederick, sought his pleasure!

He sat up, settled his hat, and wrote out the commission.

As he was putting his signature to it, a crimson reflection from the window flickered across the paper. The sound of wheels came on, repeated at short intervals, accompanied by flashes of light. The clock struck eight, and on the stroke entered Strützky, the *Kammerhussar,* bearing supper. It consisted of a concentrated bouillon, boiling hot, and two saucers, one of powdered mace, the other of ginger. The King dealt the spices by spoonfuls into the boiling hot drink, clasped the cup with both hands, and tossed off the contents. This was his notion of hygiene.

All this time the rolling of wheels went on, and the reflection of flames.

"What's going on outside there, do you

know?" Frederick inquired. For at this hour of night the castle square was wont to lie in darkness and silence.

The *Kammerhussar* made an embarrassed face. But he gave the explanation.

The capital had been holding its breath for days over the Arnold affair. This afternoon's event had circulated swiftly, and general indignation and sympathy were felt for the judges who had been placed under arrest. But to the fallen Chancellor the world of fashion gave an ovation: with torch-lit carriages, "Society" drove in a long procession past the house of that popular man and paid him homage — and took expressly the route past the castle, certainly not the shortest one.

Frederick stumped to the window, to look at the show. Without undue excitement, with a little languid curiosity and a little mocking sympathy, he looked down into the square, as a neglected old father gazes on the doings of his dashing children, of whom he holds no great opinion.

"Come," he said after a little, "fetch me to

32

bed." Strützky held the light.

The sleeping-chamber was next door. Strützky carefully pulled off the King's old clothes
and bound a woollen scarf about his head. The
pain had come on again. He sank in a sitting
posture on the edge of the bed. "Never mind,"
he said weakly, when the other, with his head
turned away, would have reached him another
shirt; "I can sleep in the one I have on."

He stretched himself out, with a groan.
Strützky spread the covers over him, waited
to hear if there were further commands, then
let himself down on one knee, made a show of

33

kissing the King's hand, put out the light, and left the room.

The King lay on his back, one knee bent in the posture he knew was kindest to it; the left, the suffering hand intricately laid to rights beneath the covers. The pain grew less in the warmth. All at once he felt very tired. His small face, grotesquely framed in the woollen scarf, was turned up to the ceiling. He went to sleep.

At lengthening intervals the carriages still rattled over the square, belated participants who would not be behind in civic spirit. Every now and then the light from the torches came through the thin curtains and fell bloodily across the sleeping face. But at length the last one passed. No more came.

34

The Cicatrice

1

As he had risen at three, and at noon, contrary to his habit, had not lingered at table, his day's work was now, at two o'clock, very nearly done. Remained the audience to the Austrian envoy, appointed for five o'clock; this a matter of form only, for the War of the Bavarian Succession was inevitable.

He began it with distaste. His grey old age, he had thought, should be free from bloody adventures. He lacked his early joy in arms, lacked the unbroken will to power; was far too experienced and cynical to have retained the

37

mental simplicity which can rejoice in warlike deeds. Here was merely question of a trouble-some necessity.

Misgivings he had none. He knew his army,

and knew through spies, whom he used un-scrupulously, the military condition of Aus-tria as well. He would certainly reach his goal. In the direction his life had taken he could tolerate no Austrian preponderance. But he was sated beforehand with success: what greater things could come to him now, at the end of his days? He was weary. If he examined himself more nearly, he discovered a regret that he must spend another summer out there in Moravia or Bohemia, amid dirt and noise, instead of here in his "vineyard," his peaceful habitation. How many summers were left him for Sans Souci, ailing as he was, and worn out with his sixty-six years? It was on purpose to have something of the spring that he had come out earlier than usual from the palace at Potsdam, and the sun seemed to mean well by him, for these April days were rarely lovely.

He had had a comfortable deep arm-chair with a sloping back brought out on the terrace and sat now before the middle entrance of his villa, wearing the blue coat of his first infantry guard regiment, almost without decorations; on his head the hat which nowadays he scarcely ever took off except at table. His legs he had put up on a low tabouret to keep them from the damp, and across his knees lay the sable pelisse trimmed with silver braid which he had once received as a present from the Empress

39

Elizabeth, the one costly article in his ward-robe, and now, like his other clothing, worn thin and shabby. Close beside him, the favourite in his lap, two others in the sun on the ground, the Italian greyhounds lay and blinked and sniffed comically in the lucent but still coolish air. She, the favourite, sniffed at his left breast-pocket, for it was there he usually kept the little tablets of chocolate with which she was often regaled.

Just now he was occupied with other matters. He was reading in a beautifully printed book bound in pink morocco. It was a French translation of Lucretius, but only the first part, for his hands were sometimes so weak from gout that he could not hold heavy volumes and they had to be dismembered for him.

He read—as how often before!—the third book of Lucretius, probably dearer to him than any poesy else in all the world: that poem which dealt with extinction in death, of the cessation of the consciousness and therewith of all evil; of the silent bliss of nothingness. Long ago this poetry had become for him the source

of his consolation. That sickly private citizen of Rome who, eighteen centuries before, in his little villa on the Aventine, had written this majestic hymn in praise of annihilation, stood for the King in the room of all the preachers and teachers of salvation who glorify the dignity and the immortality of the soul. No, not everlastingly had man to struggle and endure!

The King read, the book close to his eyes, for he was very short-sighted, and his lips shaped noiselessly the languid flow of the French verse. Yes, it must have quite a different sound in the powerful beat of the Latin dactyls! Once he had tried to read the original text, but soon gave up discouraged. His Latin was a wretched affair, it was not nearly enough; and though from year to year he told himself he would take it up again, he was secretly well enough aware that in this life he would never find the time. Was not this present hour the last for very long that he would have for his beloved books and his fruitful solitude? Ah, it was scarcely fruitful any more!

He left off reading, and clapped open his

42

lorgnon to look at the distant scene. His eye
followed the long line beginning at the flight
of steps and continued on the other side of the
fountains—which, to his sorrow, never played
—by the broad lime-tree avenue. The first
fresh shimmer of life lay over everything. The
avenue ended in front of the charming house
occupied by his friend, the old man who was
so much older even than himself. Here they

43

lived facing each other, eye in eye, and if they had not been so old, they might literally have seen each other. But such sight they no longer had.

He let his lorgnon fall, and brooded. A deep, enchanting stillness reigned.

All at once the greyhounds sprang up and began to howl. They were used, out here, to peace and quiet, and angrily gave tongue when a strange presence announced itself in the spacious garden.

The King peered across and made out a bustling, over there at the house of his friend. He blinked and strained his gaze through the glass; a litter was coming, borne by servants in bright-coloured clothes. George Keith, Earl Marischal of Scotland, was approaching.

2

THE visit was unexpected, for it was months now since the aged man had left his house — latterly the King had gone to him instead. Ancient he was, well-nigh mythically old, surely over ninety; the King liked to bring up the fact that when he, Frederick, was born, Keith had already fought under Marlborough in Flanders, not as an apprentice to the trade of arms, but already with the rank of brigadier-general.

His life, a life of the highest, most exemplary loyalty, filled a century. He had, Scot of Scots that he was, hereditary grand marshal of his country, fought for the Pretender James against the House of Hanover, given himself to the Stuart cause with more of fervour and constancy than the Stuarts themselves. England had proscribed him, confiscated his property, sentenced him to death. Almost his whole life he had spent in exile, in Venice, in Rome, in southern France, a long time in Spain; al-

45

ways given to great causes, a little consoled for the loss of his native land by the benignity of warmer suns.

How painfully he must miss these here, Frederick was driven to think, as he watched the colourful little troop coming slowly up the almost leafless avenue! It had been a piece of royal self-will to keep him. Lord Marischal had served him, had been his ambassador to Paris in a critical time, also governor in Neuf-châtel. But most valuable of all, most indispensable, he had become during the fourteen years in which, quite simply the King's friend, he had lived here close by. He was fine, he was upright, and he had *esprit:* a combination the King had not found elsewhere in the course of a long life, and so did his utmost to bind to himself this venerable man.

The low, pleasant house from which he was now being carried had been built by Frederick expressly for him. He alone had the right to come up the terraces to Sans Souci whenever he liked. He did not need to announce himself even for meals; if a large company was bidden,

46

he was still the most honoured guest; if but two or three closer friends, none could be closer or come more opportunely. One of the guest-chambers on the left side of the house, west of the domed salon, stood always ready for the old man, where he might rest after a meal; the meal itself always contained, if possible, some favourite dish of his, and the King himself served him to it.

"Aren't your legs good for it any more, my old lord," thought Frederick, "that you must have your heathen carry you this little way?" He kept the lorgnon before his eyes and thought he made out, within the little vehicle, the pronounced features of his old friend. In this affection probably deceived him; what he did actually recognize was the dress the figure wore: a black velvet housecoat, braided like a hussar's jacket and trimmed at throat and sleeves with brown fur. On the head was a soft, drooping bonnet, in shape very like a Phrygian cap. And he recognized the bearers: it was the Moor and the Tibetan. They stepped along cautiously in their gay attire.

For the household over which the Scottish
nobleman presided was quaintly composed.
"My little Tartar horde," he was used to call

his domestic staff—and in fact hardly one of
his retinue was a baptized Christian. They
came of all nations: some he had brought back
with him from his travels, some were prisoners
of war given him by his brother James, the

Commander-in-Chief. But they lived as freemen in his house, and if one of them wanted to go home, Lord Marischal did not object, but even made the arrangements. It seldom happened, for all his infidels looked up to him as a father. And he thought of them as his children, he addressed them as equals, and this — most amazing of all — only made them reverence him the more.

For a few minutes now the tiny cortège was not visible: the steps were too steep and it was climbing the side slope. Frederick smiled, with a parting glance at the volume of Lucretius; then he got up, not without difficulty, to meet his friend, for the foremost of the exotic bearers — it was the Moor — now appeared over the edge of the terrace.

3

THE old earl got out. As he stood there, in his velvet shoes, his fragility was displayed to the full. The King, himself so fragile and weary, offered his arm, and led his friend slowly across the gravelled terrace to the door.

"I felt I wanted to come, my King," he said, "and have all this before my eyes once more." He halted and turned his gaze to the steps. "It is true I do not see much of it, but I know that once I did see it all from here: the lovely slopes and the statues and over there my house, and beyond, the spreading plain and the river."

He spoke a difficult, faltering French, spoke even his mother tongue but slowly. His enunciation, however, was not due to a labouring brain, but to an unusual degree of conscientiousness. His hesitation and feeling for words had a charm of its own; precisely in French, that ripples in the rule so stintlessly on, the careful seeking often led to unexpected and enchantingly naïve turns of speech.

"You wanted to come once more, you say?" asked King Frederick, as together they entered the domed salon. "You know, my dear lord, that my vineyard is as much yours as mine. Even when I am not here, you must come whenever you choose."

Keith made no reply. He looked about the lofty oval room, through whose skylight the yellow April sun was falling. Here often in his younger years he had sat at dinner with the King, among a lively company. His brother James, the Commander-in-Chief, would be across the table, the doors and windows wide open to the summer without. They sat as though in the open air — and, to enhance the blithe illusion, the floor was inlaid with gay-coloured wreaths of vine.

He looked down on these marble garlands, now a little dim; next his weak eyes sought out the portrait bronze of Charles the Twelfth, which he had always faced as he sat at table. He looked at the intrepid brow, and the unstable mouth. Then he let himself be led forward.

In the room on the right, the first of the King's personal suite of four, he paused before a beautiful large table, inlaid with agate. He ran his wizened hand across the top; also over a costly vase of some precious stone with light-coloured stripes, that had always pleased his fancy.

"I wanted to see it all once more," he re-

iterated. "Pray bear with me, my King." Never since his native Stuarts had betrayed their dignity in exile, had he called him anything else. "My good lord," the King addressed him in return.

In the music-room he paused again, before the green marble chimney-piece. But here he neither touched nor looked at anything. He gazed downwards, with a mild expression of the sunken eyes. Frederick looked at his profile: the powerful nose projected strikingly from the lean, wrinkled face, and the chin was that of a stalwart, resolute man. But strength, spirit, and manhood were gone; not much was left for death to extinguish.

Keith seemed to listen in the calm air of the music-room. "My King," he said, in his deliberate way, "I hear music. I hear it rather better than if it were played. I have no longer any legs, I have no longer any eyes, I have no longer any ears."

"You don't miss much," said Frederick. "Neither could I make music for you — I cannot hold the flute for gout. We are fine fellows, we two."

"You cannot compare yourself with me, my King. A man of your age might be my son."

Frederick smiled. "Why not say I myself might be your son?" he asked. "Or would you turn courtier in your old age, my good lord? But you are right, most Kings are fools: they forget that their first home too was nowhere else than between the bladder and the rectum."

They entered the sleeping-chamber, a large alcoved room. In the recess stood the simple bed, shut off by a grille of gilded bronze. On the mantelshelf was a small antique bust of Marcus Aurelius, the noble head of white marble, the robe of polychrome agate.

"My King," Keith said, "I should like to hold that in my hands." Frederick took it down, not without some trouble, and set it on a little table, and the old man felt gently over it. "*Vertueux Marc-Aurèle, l'exemple des humains, mon héros, mon modèle,*'" said he as he felt, in his Scottish accents. They were Frederick's own lines, quoted from a dream picture of himself, and he divined from whom the old earl took leave, while his hands held the bust encompassed.

He was greatly touched. He took the old lord again by the arm, and tried to speak; but was so unused to expressing any emotion that he made several false starts. At last he said — and had to say it very loud, for Keith was really almost deaf:

56

"My dear lord, I have experienced so much the faithlessness and the ingratitude of men, I might be forgiven for losing faith in the human heart. But you force me to believe in it again."

He cleared his throat and together they passed through the little corridor into the library.

57

4

It was the last room in the suite, a small circular chamber wainscoted in cedar. Here deathly stillness always reigned. In shallow glass cases were the King's books, uniformly and exquisitely bound in red with gold tooling — a choice collection of French literature and the important classical authors; also Italian, English, and Spanish books in translations. There was not a German author among them. Tables heaped with papers stood about. Four antique busts looked down from lofty consoles: Homer, Socrates, Apollo, and an unnamed philosopher. The two windows reached to the ceiling and almost to the floor. One of them, on the front, looked across the slopes and gardens to the Havel, while the other gave on the east, with a close view of the beautiful bronze youth with his arms above his head, the so-called Antinous, and the reclining Flora caressed by Amor.

The King seated the old marshal in the seat

58

commanding a view of the statuary, a little sofa that stood in a niche in the wall. He glanced outside and saw the litter where the

old earl had left it, and motionless beside it the Tibetan and the Moor. The Moor wore a scarlet jacket and a sort of primitive turban wound round his head. The Tibetan was clad in yel-

59

low, with a peaked hat which somehow betrayed that it had not come out of Asia, but rather been fashioned from memory by unskilful hands. There stood the two, right and left of the carrying-chair, and stared upon the gravel path.

The King was amused. "Look at your servants standing there," he laughed. "Why don't they talk to each other?"

"They cannot, my King. Neither can understand a single word the other says. Oh, in my house it is marvellous! The servants can't understand each other, they only understand me. And each of them has a different religion."

"Yes," said Frederick, whom the mere word always irritated. "Every people has thought itself out its own particular foolishness."

"Oh, I don't mind about that. If they are contented and decent in this life, they may think what they like about another one. A few weeks since, one evening at sunset, I went into the room where they stop together; and there I saw a singular sight."

"They were at their devotions, my lord?"

60

"Yes. But each one a different kind. There stood Hanghi the Tibetan, turning a sort of child's rattle round in his hand, a little mill he called it, and every time it turned was as good as a prayer. In a corner on his knees was Ibra-

him the Tartar, praising Allah and the Prophets. And Stephan the Kalmuk stood upright, his hands over his eyes, and prayed without making a sound."

"And the Negro — what was he doing?"

"The Negro was standing in the middle of the room and goggling," said Keith. "I don't know what he was thinking. In point of fact, he always goggles."

"Yes," Frederick said, "he's goggling now. I'll tell them to go get something to eat."

He opened the window and gave an order. The two outside made obeisance, but did not stir from their place.

Keith laughed until the deep wrinkles in his old face opened out. He shouted a few barbaric-sounding words, and the servants ran off behind the house in the direction of the kitchen. The litter, with its covering of light-blue cloth, stood on the terrace, whence the sun seemed to have withdrawn. Keith shivered.

"Forgive me, my good lord," said Frederick and pulled the bell, "we must have a fire at once." Neumann the hussar appeared and heaped up wood in the chimney.

"Thanks, my King," said Keith. "If I may say so, you owe me this fire. Ah," he went on, "in Spain I had good friends, but, after all, my best one was the sun!"

"What you tell me about it always sounds like a fairy tale. At bottom one can only believe in what one sees; and remember, I have seen nothing! Old man that I am, I have never travelled, never could travel."

This melancholy strain of his friend the old

earl knew well. Rather more briskly than usual
he resumed:

"It may be better for you, my King, that my
time will soon be up, that I shall surely never
go more to Spain. Else I should denounce you
to the Holy Office for witchcraft! For you must
have bewitched me, or how could I have
stopped here under this leaden sky, when I
might have lived and died in the lovely climate
of Valencia?"

"You speak in every sentence of dying,
Keith. But I expect to find you alive and
hearty when I come back from my travels."

"Then, faith, they must be short ones — and
that such 'travels' as yours are not very likely
to be! No, no, my works are running down."

Frederick gainsaid him no more. The pretence was distasteful to them both. "The simile
of the timepiece is quite correct," he said. "I
thought of it myself just lately, when the
clock in the tower of that tiresome Garrison
Church had to be renewed. It is made of steel
and iron, and yet it doesn't last more than
twenty years; but a man, a thing put together

63

out of mud and spittle, he wants to last four times as long? There's no sense to it."

5

THERE came a scratch at the door, and the *Kammerhussar* appeared with a large wicker basket full of fruit. At the King's express order, the yield of his glass-houses was brought to him daily — he took especial pleasure in fine tropical fruit.

It was offered to the old marshal, and he took a banana.

"Don't blame me, my lord, if it is pithy! My conservatories are kept as hot as the bad place, but it seems as though mere contact with our soil makes the seeds shrivel. My poor oranges and lemons and olives — they all die of starvation in this desert."

"One southern plant," Keith said quite low, "has flourished here: the laurel."

"O, Keith, Keith!" cried Frederick, and laughed. "One might think you were after an order!" He went on vivaciously: "What is there I have not tried? I have pursued the gardeners, Georgics in hand: I have supervised digging and sowing and planting — and always they say to me: 'That is all foolishness, that is no way to go to work.' Alas, for this climate and this soil what Virgil can arise?"

"The Georgics," ruminated Keith. "I don't know them either, any more. I have utterly forgotten them. My memory fails now day by day."

"There is a remedy for that: I stir a spoonful of white mustard in my coffee every day now, it strengthens the memory."

"I should not care for the taste of it, my King. And I don't even care any longer to strengthen my memory. They read aloud a good deal to me nowadays, out of my favourite books: Tacitus, Swift, Montaigne, sometimes out of *Don Quixote;* and it is all quite new to me, I hear it as though for the first time. And that is a boon conferred upon me by my great age — about the only one."

"Do not repine, my Lord Keith. You have had a good life. Or tell me how you would have arranged it if you were what they call a god, and had the power."

66

"How I would arrange it? Let me think. Up to thirty years, I would choose to be a pretty woman; up to sixty a victorious general, and then — then —"

"Then surely the Earl Marischal after that!"

"No, after that a cardinal in Rome."

"My good lord," said Frederick, "you are giving me one surprise after another today. First you come out as a courtier, then as a pious and god-fearing man."

Again they were interrupted. This time it was one of the private secretaries; as usual at this midday hour, the letters and rescripts drawn up by the King in the early morning were brought to him for his signature.

With the functionary the greyhounds rushed into the room again. "Who said you might come, rascals?" Frederick addressed them. They recognized the friendly tone and leaped and fawned upon him. The King did not greet the secretary at all; but the old marshal lifted himself on his stick and bowed with great courtesy.

"Lay it all there on the table," Frederick

67

said in German to the man, "and give me the address to the generals. You will get it printed at the usual place."

"Yes, Your Majesty."

"But on no account before I've delivered it."

"Certainly not, Your Majesty."

"I deliver it Tuesday or Wednesday, so you must not print it before Thursday. If you do, you will have to answer to me!"

"Yes, Your Majesty."

"You have to repeat everything a dozen times, my lord," he turned to Keith. "They are all such Bœotians."

The secretary went very red. But the marshal smiled at him out of his mild eyes, and with his flaccid mouth, so benignly that the chidden one knew he need feel no shame before this good old man.

The King held the sheet of paper in his hands. He had dictated the text, and this was the translation.

"We still have to make military speeches, no matter how old we are!" he said to Keith. "It's a fine trade! You will laugh, my lord, to find me

68

as full of pathos as a hero of Corneille. Well, well, let's hold a dress rehearsal. Come on, little ones," he said to the greyhounds, who stood round him expectantly wagging their tails. "You shall be my generals. Form a line there. You, Phryne, are General Stutterheim, you, Pompon, are General Moellendorf; and you, Rabbitfoot, are General Butra."

Keith laughed heartily, the secretary's face preserved its solemn, woebegone look. And the King read; he read in his clear, ringing tones, giving the German a foreign intonation, as he always did, and speaking rather loud so that the old marshal might understand it all, for at bottom Frederick was very proud of this composition of his.

" 'Gentlemen, most of us have served together since our young days, we have grown grey in the service of the Fatherland and we know each other perfectly well. The hardships and agitations of war we have already shared, honourably and to the utmost, and I am aware that you dislike as much as I do the shedding of blood. But my empire is in danger.'

69

"One always has to say that, my lord," he threw in, but added at once, "and at bottom it is true too."

"'It is my duty as the King to protect my subjects, and to act with the utmost swiftness and display of strength in order to avert if possible the storm which threatens them. To this end, gentlemen'"—he looked solemnly at his dogs—"'I count upon your zeal in the service and your affection to my person, which you have at all times evinced, and which has never

been without its effect. Moreover you may be assured that I shall continue to recognize with warm and fervent gratitude the services which you render to your Fatherland and your King.' "

With the last words he groped in his breast-pocket and brought out some little cakes of chocolate. The greyhounds were still squatting in a circle at attention; but on receiving the reward "for their services" they abandoned their pose and fell to nibbling at their charming ease.

The King's tone changed altogether. " 'I will also beg you,' " he said, seriously, " 'not to forget your humanity when the foe is in your power, but to exact the strictest discipline from your troops. I shall march'—Oh, no, no," he said to the secretary, "not march, nothing about marching. *'Je pars'* was what I dictated, and what I dictated is good enough for you. Give me a pencil!" He made the correction and went on reading:

" 'I am now about to set out. But I do not ask to travel like a king. Fine equipages have no

71

charms for me. My infirm age, however, will not let me travel as I did in my fiery youth. I must avail myself of a post-chaise, and you are at liberty to do the same. But on the field of battle you will see me on horseback, and therein, I hope, my generals will follow my example.' "

He affixed his signature to the sheet and handed it back. "For if the Austrian gentleman were to come now and find it lying on the table, he would turn straight round again — and that, considering all the rhetoric he has got ready, would be a pity."

The secretary went out, and the greyhounds had to go with him. "They would open hostilities prematurely. They bit the buckle off the Russian plenipotentiary's breeches the other day — they are quite mad. Yes, yes, Pompon, it was you did it, you must go along with the others."

And he shut the door behind them.

6

THE King was in a baroque mood — and it was not a pleasant one. It relished him, one moment to revise this address, which was the opening gun of the war, and in the next, as though there still existed any chance of composition, to receive the envoy of the opposed power.

"You will now see me before you in the rôle of hypocrite," he said, with a hard glitter in his eye. He disappeared, and brought out of the music-room a small but speaking likeness of the Emperor Joseph, which stood there on a chest of drawers. He set it up on the mantel-shelf, in the best light in the room.

"Not such a bad face, really," said he. "Or don't you think so, Keith?"

"He looks like a sensible man, and like a good one, too."

"And yet he is the one who is urging on this war. He is ambitious. Well, that is natural. Theresa doesn't want it, she is in a great fright. She is afraid of having to roast a thousand years longer in purgatory. And besides, she already knows the looks of my whiskers. They say she gets in a great taking when she sets eyes on a blue uniform."

He glanced down at his coat and a sudden thought seemed to strike him. He pulled at the bell-rope.

"Watch, my lord, you shall see me put on a mask."

"You are a courtly monarch, you mean to offer your guests some entertainment."

"Hark ye," Frederick said to the hussar as he entered; "that white coat I wore in Neustadt must still be in my wardrobe. Fetch it hither." The servant went out.

"That's seven years ago, already," said Frederick. "It was the first time I met young Joseph officially. Kaunitz was there too. He is a great ass, but a fox too. We all of us had white coats made, to spare the Austrians the sight of the hated blue—ah, there it is! Look here, my lord!"

And Frederick got into the white coat, which was patterned more or less on the Austrian

74

regimentals, and embroidered with silver. It became him very oddly indeed. Neumann bore the Prussian coat back into the bedroom.

"This splendid coat ought by rights to have a splendid order on it. And you will see, Keith,

75

the Austrian count will wear the Golden
Fleece. I always have to laugh when I see it.
Why should a man want to carry a dead sheep
round on his chest?"

"In any case, my King, your toilet is now
complete, and the Ambassador of the Holy
Roman Empire will be coming." He prepared
to rise.

"What do you mean? Do you think I will
give up the pleasure of your company for the
sake of these letter-carriers? And besides," he
added, "Graf Cobenzl won't be alone, either.
He is bringing a secretary with him, who is to
be presented. Funny idea, that, on the eve of
a war. Most likely a spy. These legation secretaries are all spies."

"He won't have much luck, in your domains."

"There are rascals everywhere. But at all
events, there are no court ladies here, no princesses for a young gallant like that to lead on
till they tell everything they know."

Keith laughed. "I had the impression," he
said, "just between ourselves, that Your Maj-

76

esty pretty frequently made use of the same weapons."

"My lord is very clever indeed, but he is mistaken there. They cost too much. These secretaries use up unholy amounts in flowers and sweets and carriages; and as a rule nothing comes of it. No, I have confined myself to corrupting the ladies' maids. For that you only need fine lusty lower-class lads, who are never suspected of being in my pay. They get their five hundred thaler a year and have a glorious good time into the bargain, the young gallowsbirds! Their reports aren't so well spelt, maybe, but there's more to them."

The hussar appeared, and in a loud voice announced the Austrian gentlemen.

7

Count Ludwig Cobenzl, plenipotentiary of Their Roman and Apostolic Majesties, entered the room. He was still quite a young man, with a cool, alert cast of countenance, dressed with great elegance in white and orange. Sure enough, he wore upon his breast the Order of the Golden Fleece. With him was a slim, handsome young man of about his own age, southern in type, likewise elegantly dressed, or even with more magnificence than himself. Both made courtly bows.

"How do you do, sir?" said the King, and even took off his greasy uniform hat—which certainly did not go with his costume. "I am enchanted to see you."

"Your Majesty has graciously permitted that I introduce my companion—herewith—and humbly present him: the noble Calsabigi, formerly in the service of Their Majesties in Naples, now sent hither from Vienna as envoy extraordinary."

78

"Ah, very good," said Frederick. "The gentlemen must not be disturbed if His Lordship the Hereditary Grand Marshal of Scotland is — herewith — present at our interview. He is my friend — I have no secrets from him."

The old earl bowed, more perfunctorily, it is

true, than he had previously to the secretary. He had seen, in his lifetime, so many ministers and ambassadors! Neither were the monarchs whom these two represented the objects of his special regard. "What is a crown, after all?" he was used to say. "Only a hat that lets the rain through on top."

Meanwhile the Ambassador had been looking about him. His gaze roved from the King's white coat to the portrait of his master in the

79

place of honour on the chimney-piece; and probably he knew not what to make of these phenomena. Young Calsabigi fixed upon the King's face a gaze melting with admiration.

"You are surprised, perhaps," the King opened the interview, in the lightest of tones, "to see me in your coat. It is the one I wore when I met your sovereign."

Cobenzl bowed.

"But in private you are probably thinking that I am not truly worthy to wear your colours. I am not so clean as you Austrians." He pointed down at the white silk, that was snuff-stained from top to bottom. At the same time he took a sizable pinch from one of the jewelled snuff-boxes that stood about.

"Your Royal Majesty," began the diplomat, "affords me the liveliest pleasure by showing yourself in our colours. Your Majesty is pleased to jest over small stains which your coat has acquired in service; but the fact that I see it today upon Your Royal Majesty fills my heart with the hope that Your Majesty will not blacken it with powder."

"That is very well put, Cobenzl. And yet there is something wrong with it. For when I start shooting I wear the other, the blue one. But a truce to compliments," he went on. "Let me hear your embassy."

"Your Majesty," Cobenzl began, "will permit me to say at once that only a portion of the mission from Vienna has been put into my mouth today. An essential part, perhaps the more important, has been entrusted to the *Nobile* Calsabigi here, as a special mission — I do not even know whether by Her Majesty the Queen-Empress or His Majesty the Roman Emperor."

Calsabigi bowed, with a magnificent sweep of his fine figure:

"Yes," Frederick said, and wrinkled his brows, "I know how the thing stands. Your young Kaiser wants the war, your old Kaiserin doesn't. She has said herself that the Viennese claims are superannuated, and not very well established. If she sees that, then she ought to get her co-regent to listen to reason. But where do I come in?"

He half turned to the Italian as he spoke. The latter answered, in a velvety baritone, with exotically coloured vowels:

"Your Royal Majesty, those in high places think to have found a way that will be pleasing to all the high contracting parties, and wound the susceptibilities of none."

"Susceptibilities? We are not dealing with susceptibilities, but with interests. And my interests will be uninjured only if they are prepared in Vienna for immediate evacuation of the Bavaria they unlawfully occupy. If they are prepared to do that, then you may perfectly well tell me so in the presence of his Lordship and the Ambassador here. If not, then I see no reason why I should receive you in special audience."

It was brusque. Calsabigi quivered the lids of his speaking eyes, and said meekly: "Your Majesty robs me of a great pleasure, for which I had been ardently longing."

Frederick turned to Keith and cut a grimace. The old man, in all probability, did not see it. Then he addressed himself once more to

Cobenzl, and formally demanded his mission. The count, despite his youth a finished diplomat — at twenty he had been Austria's plenipotentiary in Copenhagen — delivered himself with clarity, in unexceptionable form. He had, of course, nothing new to say.

In a French worthy of the Tuileries he put the claims of the House of Habsburg to a large part of Bavaria — the very claims on which the Queen herself had cast doubts, as not being fully borne out by facts. In Cobenzl's mouth they were, by every legal system and statute, indefeasible. He recapitulated the terms of the family compact which twelve years before Max Joseph had made with the landless Kurfürst

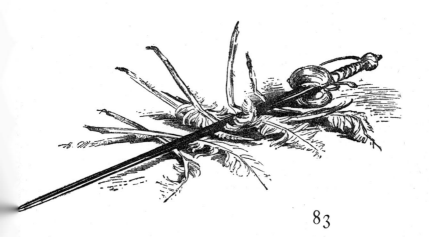

Karl Theodore of the Palatinate; he mentioned in passing, almost in an aside, the later attempt to bring in the Duke of Zweibrücken, the heir presumptive; he reminded them of the death of Max Joseph, which had taken place the year before. . . .

"We all know he's dead, Cobenzl," Frederick said peevishly; "don't beat about the bush like that."

The envoy, not visibly taken aback, continued: mentioned that Karl Theodore, the present ruler of Bavaria, had explicitly and voluntarily recognized the claims of the House of Habsburg, and, Cobenzl added, this prince was after all the person most concerned.

"Wrong," said Frederick. "The person most concerned is the Duke of Zweibrücken, whose children and children's children should one day reign over Bavaria."

"Surely," Cobenzl countered, "the only reason the Kurfürst recognized the Austrian claims was because he could not conceal from himself that they were valid."

"Surely," said Frederick, "it was more because he has a troop of illegitimate children, and wants the Emperor to give them titles and dowries. Why do you keep quiet, Cobenzl, about things we all of us know perfectly well? It's that sort of thing makes politics such a tiresome job."

They were close together in the little, no longer very light room: the King of Prussia, the Scottish hereditary grand marshal, the Belgian-born Austrian envoy, and the too-too-exquisite fourth. With short steps, his hands folded upon his white back, Frederick began to walk up and down.

"You see, Cobenzl," he began, almost affably, "if I were to follow you in the accepted key, what I should do now would be to deliver a lofty and moving discourse. And after that I should say: the point at issue is whether the Emperor is entitled to dispose of the fiefs of the Empire as he sees fit. The whole question is whether these fiefs shall be benefices, after the Turkish fashion, good only for life, and devisable again by the Sultan after the death of an incumbent. No, I should say, that contradicts the laws and usages of the Roman Empire, and no imperial German prince could reconcile it with his honour. I myself, I should say, feel as a member of the Roman Empire and as a German prince. I renewed the Peace of Westphalia by the Peace of Hubertusburg, and as a high contracting party to that peace I am, I should say, bound to protect the rights of the princely houses of Germany against any encroachment by the head of the Empire."

He paused before the Ambassador.

"That, Cobenzl, is what I should say if I wanted to make diplomatic rhetoric. If I were to compose an official letter to your Kaiser, it would have to be couched in some such terms. Letters like that get put in the archives and then in the history-books, and after a while they serve as text for schoolboys. But to you, Cobenzl, I say that I cannot tolerate the annexation of Bavaria, because it would mean too large an accretion to the Habsburg power; also, because it would endanger my hereditary claims to Bayreuth and Anspach."

The King seemed as though he would conclude at this point. "My sovereign," began the envoy, "is quite prepared—"

"Tut, tut, Cobenzl. He is quite prepared to guarantee my claims. He thinks, and he is perfectly right, that I am a worn-out old man, and the devil will soon fly away with me. And after that everything will fall out as he wants it. He is young, the future is his. I am aware that personally your sovereign feels cordially toward me—he has evinced the feeling chiefly by making a thorough study of my life. Now he thinks to strengthen the power of his dynasty, precisely as I did mine early in my career, and to make good the loss of Silesia. He thinks I ought to let him carry out his plan, since it would not be at my expense. But it *would* be at my expense, Cobenzl, or at least I think it would, and old fellows like me are obstinate."

With his last words Frederick had turned away toward the side window. The day had grown dull and leaden. Outside there the beautiful bronze youth lifted his hands to the grey heavens like one anguishing in exile; the Flora looked as though she had flung herself down in a pet. 87

Cobenzl waited to see if the King would not turn round. He exchanged a look with his companion. Then he said:

"Your Royal Majesty! The special mission entrusted in Vienna to the *Nobile* Calsabigi is of course unknown to me. But I may confidently assume that he is the bearer of quite personal assurances from the highest quarters, of which not even the Cabinet has been informed, nor Prince Kaunitz—"

Frederick had left his window. "Prince Kaunitz," he said briskly, and his tones were glib and chatty, "amused me, rather, that time in Neustadt. He is indisputably a man of spirit and has very fine gifts; but he has a weakness of taking himself for an oracle and everybody else for a fool. Of me, he thought I was just a soldier, with no head for politics. Yes, he amused me a good deal," he concluded, and his tone betrayed satisfaction, he felt sure he had put the envoy off his train of thought.

But now something wholly unexpected happened. The noble Calsabigi made an impetuous stride toward the King; he flung himself at his

88

feet and embraced one of the old top-boots that
showed beneath the silver-embroidered hem of
the Austrian coat-skirts.

"Your Majesty!" he cried, beseechingly, ardently. "Of your infinite mercy grant me the
crowning joy of the interview I seek. Since I
was a boy, Your Majesty has been my idol,
the glowing axle round which turned all my
thoughts and deeds. The blissfullest day of my
life was that on which they entrusted me in
Vienna with a mission to the great Prussian
King. In the dust I implore you, let me lay it
before Your Royal Majesty, and thus may it
be vouchsafed me to serve as an instrument, to
the end that peace and concord may prevail between the two exalted houses!"

As Calsabigi lay, neither the old marshal nor
the young envoy could see his face. He raised
his beautiful, doglike eyes to Frederick's, and
the startled, even embarrassed monarch read in
their gaze that which enlightened him in a twin-
kling. For their gaze was not imploring, it was
not servile adoration they expressed; what he
read in them was vice, was prurience, seduction.

89

And Calsabigi's two hands were gently caressing his leg in the old boot, from the elaborately dressed hair rose a subtle perfume, a female aroma.

Frederick took a backward step; so suddenly that the kneeling man pitched forward to the floor, and rested his weight an instant on his hands.

"I have said what I have to say, Count Cobenzl," said Frederick. "If you wish to ask for your passport, it is at your service. You take with you my personal regard, and the conviction that you will yet perform worthy service for your country. I regret that further conversations between us are useless; they are, with persons who abuse my royal presence, also impossible. I will write your sovereign a letter, the content of which shall be the things we have been saying. But I will write it in the field. Gentlemen, I wish you adieu!"

The Ambassador, silenced, confounded, left the room. Calsabigi followed, utterly crushed, not even venturing a farewell. Earl Marischal did not rise as they went out.

"Ah, Keith, Keith!" cried Frederick. Disgust and desperation strove together in his face. He even made as though to flee toward the old man for refuge, but collected himself and stood still.

Keith directed upon the King his honourable old eyes.

"My King," he said, mildly, "what have they done? What is it makes Your Majesty so over-wrought?"

8

HE got no immediate reply, Frederick pulled at the bell-rope.

"My old coat, my good, honest old coat," he cried to the hussar. He flung off the white garment and stood there for a few moments in his shirtsleeves and yellow waistcoat. "Here," he cried, having donned the blue uniform and hat once more, "here, take this thing, run into the kitchen with it. His Lordship's two menservants are there. One of them is a black man. Make him a present of it. But he is not to put it on to carry my lord in the litter nor to do other honourable service, only when he is washing up or cleaning out drains — but wait, I forget, he won't understand a word you say! No matter, go give it him!

"Oh, Keith, Keith," he cried again, when they were alone. "What do you say to that? They set out to seduce me, over in Vienna — me! Look at me, and then tell me if you think I look like a man that is likely to be seduced?"

He made a downward gesture, at his wasted, warped little figure in the shabby clothes. "They say kings are made in the image of God. The other day I was looking at myself in the glass and I thought to myself: 'I feel sorry for God, if that is what he looks like!' "

And he laughed. But there was neither anger nor amusement in his laugh. There was despair.

"Yes, that is the way they go about with me, my dear brothers and sisters the most Christian kings and emperors, the most Catholic, the most loyal, the most apostolic — that is the way they go about with me, the most heretical! With me, they think, everything is allowable. They want to train me away from my plans, from the steps I need to take. They want to beguile me into frailty — with whom? With a perfumed beau, a Ganymede, a male courtesan. Oh, I don't know whether it is more laughable, or sad, or disgusting!"

"My King," Earl Marischal said, slowly, "I don't understand. What is it they have done to you?"

Frederick's wrath ebbed, and he smiled. "Ah,

94

Keith, Keith," said he once more, but this time gently, as though he spoke to a beloved child. "It is a long story. After all, why should I fly into a passion? Princesses and court ladies there are none, here in my vineyard, nor even maids in waiting, for them to practise on after my thrifty prescription, so they try it on with the master of the house himself. That good, sly, pious Maria Theresa! Those sly, pious Jesuit fathers! For they would be the ones who thought up the idea, and the Empress, of course, she pretended not to understand. They picked out a fine handsome lad for me, so much is true. He was to play on my weakness till he got on the right side of me and wheedled out a few concessions to the Emperor, and on the strength of them Theresa would take it on herself to preserve the peace. It wasn't such a bad idea. I needn't have been so upset about it. After all my experience I ought to be past surprise at anything human beings can do."

"So you mean, my King," Lord Keith asked from his sofa-corner, "that they credit you with an inclination to Socratic love, and mean to

turn it to their own ends? Am I right?"

"Ah, my good lord, to ask like that one must
be a Scot, and carry a heart like yours in his
breast, and be far, far removed, in the very soul
of him, from all scandal and evil speaking. Who

96

but you could have failed to hear what all the courts have rung with, all these years?"

"My King," Keith said, "I should not have advised anyone to utter in my presence a disparaging word of you. But nobody has ever dared."

"Disparaging—I don't even know if I find it disparaging. Of Alexander it is well known, of Cæsar it is reported. And after all, Socrates with his Alcibiades is a loftier thought, it seems to me, than Jack with his Gill. Ah, my good lord, I should be better off, maybe, if what they say of me were true."

"Better off?"

The King bent his gaze on the ancient sitting there, clothed in the awe-inspiring childlikeness of his ninety years, at the end of a clean, clear course—and a feeling of mingled affection and envy came over him. How much easier Keith's life had been! Suffering and hardship, certainly, had not lacked on its long path. As a young man in Scotland he had been proscribed, hunted from village to village, from rock to rock, from island to island, a hundred times

97

threatened with a dungeon and a shameful death. Then he had had to flee his native land, after which he yearned with every drop of his honourable blood. He had seen the irreversible triumph of those who were in his eyes usurpers; and what was far harder to bear, got nothing but ingratitude and calumny from the royal house to which he had consecrated his sword and even his life. He had lost in Frederick's service his brother James, whom he dearly loved. Other blows had not been wanting; not so long ago it was, and Frederick had known of it, this man already bent with years had had another heavy grief to bear. There had been a lovely creature, a Turkish war-orphan, whom he had given a European upbringing in his house and loved like a child — and then no longer like a child. With youth's unconscious cruelty she made it clear that he was old, that life for him was finished and done.

And yet he had lived, lived a full and satisfying life. He had suffered and endured, yet known the sweets of repose; women he had embraced under every sky, both smiling and stern.

He had been a man: daring not alone in thought and deed, but also in desire and in the bliss of fulfilment.

True, immortal fame was not his lot. He would be no legend among the nations. When he went hence, and his fantastic servants bore him to the grave where he should lie, it would be an end of him; he would be no more than a pleasant and noble memory, swiftly to fade and die. He had been a wise and valiant and high-hearted gentleman, storm-tossed by life to come to haven in the affection of a king; honoured by those who served him, a bright apparition, an open book. A man, a living, breathing man. And thus to be envied.

A craving born of weakness seized on this reticent man, half numbed with his lonely life, to speak out, to unbosom himself for once. This last human being who stood near to him was now departing, soon would he be gone, already he was but the shadow of a shade.

The passage with the Italian adventurer had stirred long-buried memories in the King. Ah, how the world mistook him! Something cruel, horrible, was buried in his heart. The wound he bore — not only had it burned; far worse than that, he had been obliged to conceal it all his life, and this it was, and this alone, had cut him off from human society.

Never had he confided in anyone. Not in the mother who was dear to him as the protector of his youth, not in his clever sister of Bayreuth. All his friends, the men of intellect who had been about him, had died in ignorance of his sorest cross. On none of the thousand pages he had written about his life, in none of the thousand lines of verse in which he had gilded it with poetic glamour, was it mentioned. And that was well, it was very well. For his lot was not only hard and frightful to bear; it was hateful too — perhaps, mirrored in the vulgar understanding, it was even ridiculous.

The situation grew upon him. It had a sort of fascination. On the eve of a war, fifteen years after the last time he had led his troops under fire, on the eve of a European crisis — for the issue at stake was no less than the hegemony of the heart of the continent — and

here, for the last time, his last friend, whom he would not find again when he returned from the field with his warlike labours done.

Yes, he would speak out this once. He felt he could. Whether he would be understood was another matter; but if he were, it would all be locked within this aged breast until the day of forgetfulness so close at hand. He would speak as into a grave.

He drew up a tabouret, sat down, and took

Keith's hand, a thing he had not done in years. The King never gave his hand, even to his nearest, he avoided human contact like flames.

The marshal's hand was small and parched, like long-dried wood. Holding it, the King began to speak. Later he let it fall.

9

King Frederick, in company with men for whose minds he had respect, was witty of speech, after the manner of his century: an ornate, urbane style, rich in antithesis. But now his words were rough and curt. His phrases were bare of art, his utterance forthright. It was as though he were rolling away boulders that all these years had weighed down his soul.

"My lord," he said, "do you know how old I was when you first came to me? I was thirty-five. Was I still young? Did I seem young to you? Hardly, I think. Nor was I. My youth had long been past.

"Do you know how long it had lasted? To my twenty-first year. Then it was over.

"Had you ever thought of it, Keith? I scarcely think so. You are a faithful friend, I know it; but human beings do not think about each other. People have called Sans Souci a cloister, and Frederick its abbot; and they have laughed when they said it. But why is it a cloister, why is it different from other courts? You will say, because it pleases me to have it so. Yes, so it is.

"Hark ye, Keith; what is it man really wants? To live, and to be happy. That was what you wanted too, and you have had your wish. Your Turkish girl threw you over, and it hurt; but then you were already an old man, and what you wanted went beyond the bounds of reason.

"Well, my good lord, since I was one-and-twenty, all womankind has thrown me over. You won't understand what I say, and it is not the truth, either. I might put it that I have thrown them over — but neither is that the truth. It was Nature herself threw me over. That is the actual truth. And it was not pleasant.

"As a young man, I loved the sex beyond words. To sleep with a woman was the most glorious thing in life. For it I could have given up everything else. I need never have read a book, or mounted a horse, nor ever heard a note

of music. I could have given up all my friends,
and even my claims to the throne. But women
I must have. It began early, it got worse with

time. I saw their bosoms, I smelt their hair, and
my head would seethe as though it were dipped
in a pot of boiling water. I would lose my
senses. I had the most violent scenes with the
King, I risked my life, I thought of nothing

else. It was not love. I never was in love. No, Keith, I never saw one woman whom I could have loved. Perhaps I was too young. Perhaps it was not in me. Probably the thing is rarer than one thinks. Men tell so many lies.

"And I did not long for love. I longed for women. My father wanted to get me married. The idea did not suit me. Marriage, at twenty-one — it seemed a stupid idea. But I had no choice. I yielded, a good deal against the grain, and privately resolved not to let my wife be a hindrance to me. In all of Europe there was not one unmarried king — and certainly no faithful one.

"It was just before the wedding the thing happened. You ask me what. Well, you know, Keith, the little god with the bow" — he motioned with his head to the Flora and Amor outside — "has some poisoned arrows in his quiver. One of them hit me. I was at my wits' end. I was to marry. Precisely then I was to marry. I confided in the Margrave Heinrich, my uncle, Heinrich von Schwedt. He was my uncle, but not much older than I. The ass is alive today. You know him. I thought him prodigiously knowing. He knew what to do. It was wonderful advice he gave me. He sent me to his doctor, and a great doctor he was. Dr. von Malchow, so-called. What a duffer! I can see the fellow yet. He had a peach-coloured coat and a face like a parrot's. Parrot-faced people are always asses. He got me rid of my trouble in four days. Yes. In four days the running stopped. I was all right. I travelled to

Wolfenbüttl and we had the wedding. It was not so bad. I was quite pleased. We should certainly have had a lot of children, pure Brunswick-Bevern stock.

"After a few weeks the thing began again. The von Malchow fellow had not cured me. He had only driven the disease inwards. It broke out again. My life was endangered. Mortification was setting in. The doctors then were even stupider than they are now. I had a deadly fear of my father. I did not dare write abroad, to a really learned man. I made shift with the pack of knaves I had at hand. If they only held their tongues, that was the main thing. They operated."

The king paused. He stood up, went to the east window, and looked out. Earl Keith, already pale from being so long out of bed, stared at his back; with somewhat vacant regard he followed from the bow to the end the thin pigtail in its wrapping of brownish silk. Frederick came back and resumed his place on the tabouret, a little farther off Keith than before.

108

"After this operation I was no longer a man. I was one-and-twenty. I went back to Ruppin, to my garrison, alone.

"I was one-and-twenty. I was very sensual. I was hardly anything but sensual. I wanted to kill myself. Never, even at the most desperate crises in my wars, have I wanted so much to kill myself. But I had no poison. And maybe I had no courage either.

"The passion for women was there, but I could not gratify it. That was hideous. Hideous. So was something else. I had read the classic authors. I knew what they say of a man who is no man. Such a one, they said, loses his manliness, he is no longer brave, or magnanimous, he has neither fortitude nor candour. He becomes cowardly, petty, effeminate, crafty. I was a eunuch. A eunuch cannot be a king.

"I was a fool, I was a child. I had no one to advise me, there was no one to ask. It was all a lie. I was no eunuch. My body processes were the same, its powers, its secretions unimpaired. But I did not know it.

"It was then I fought my worst battle. Everything after that was easy by comparison. Those nights in my bed in Ruppin I fought my real wars.

"I determined to conquer nature. A few years before, I had tried to do without sleeping. I had failed. But in this I would not fail.

"They had made a eunuch of me. Very well,

I refused to be a eunuch. I would not be petty, timorous, underhanded, I would be daring, magnanimous, every inch a king. It was all nonsense. I was not in the least in danger of

altering. But now I altered myself. I had been self-indulgent. Now I became self-exacting. In winter, when I lay sleeping sound under warm covers, I would waken, get up, douse myself with water, and lie down on the ground. Whenever I had a sense of physical well-being, I thought I was getting old-womanish. And

III

that was all to the good — I owed to such fears as these everything I afterwards got done in life. All my good years I spent thus. Even when I fought my great war, I was still believing in that bogy. It is not ten years since I knew the truth.

"At twenty-eight I became king. And that made matters worse. I had an ignominious secret to guard. The scar on my body was the spur of my days. Sometimes I think it was responsible for my wars. I hurled myself into the first of them to show the world I was a man. Nights I would start up in the darkness with the thought of those physicians. Would they hold their tongues? I had no way of making them. I was a hunted man in my own house. Long before that I had sent away the Brunswick woman. I was afraid to have her look at me. I began to hate her. So I sent her away and she has been sitting there in Schönhausen ever since, without an idea why.

"I hated the whole race of womankind. And there I was, surrounded by women. All at once there were women on all the thrones of Europe:

in Vienna, St. Petersburg—even in Paris it
was not the King who reigned, it was a woman,
the sex itself.

"There were whisperings: 'How can the lord

113

of Brandenburg carry on a war, if he cannot even sleep with a woman?' I was frantic with suspicion. I heard the whisper everywhere. Once at a review two French officers are presented. I ask the name of their regiment. '*Régiment de Roussillon,*' they answer, '*autrement nommé Trousse-cotillon.*' It is meant for a witticism, and they say '*autrement.*' But I hear '*autrefois*' —and I could have strangled them.

"I did my part. I played my rôle. I was publicly unfaithful to my Brunswick spouse. I acted the infatuated before every pretty face, and got nothing but torment for my pains. I bought lascivious pictures instead of those I really liked, and had them hung so as to be always before me. I created a furore with the dancer Barberina, went about with her unmasked at the balls, and played the fool for love. Then I took her into a private room and locked the door. Inside we sat and drank tea. Yes.

"It was no good. Women cannot keep quiet. I could not command them to hold their tongues. Maybe they did, in this country. But the rogues would cross the border, and let themselves be pumped in the foreign capitals. 'There is nothing to the King of Prussia,' they said. 'He plays the gallant, but all he can do is drink tea.' And I had three women against me, three female sovereigns. All my wars I fought against women.

"Then I made up my mind. I would put a stop to the business. Men can keep their own counsel. They have to. And when they lie, the world does not necessarily believe them. I wanted nothing more ardently than to be taken for a sodomite. For if I was a sodomite, then at least I was a man.

"I succeeded. I lived in a woman's age. But it held a king who put away his wife, who kept no mistresses, associated only with men, lived among his army — well, there was the riddle, and here was the explanation. People shrank from me — but I was a man once more.

"No woman ever entered this house again. I dressed my *Kammerhussars* in short, tight-fitting clothes. My pages must be young and pretty. Early mornings I would often call one

115

into my bedroom; he had the pleasure of looking on while I got into my boots and drank my
coffee. I talked freely about Socratic love, at
table, in front of my guests, before my servants.
I have often said that the apostle John be-

longed to the brotherhood. These stories were
of course carried to Vienna. The pious Theresa
heard them. The wily Jesuit fathers heard them.
And now you know why Calsabigi fell on his
knees and did his best to beguile me. Yes, yes,
those good, saintly people!"

He gave a harsh laugh, broke off, got up, and
moved again to the window — it seemed to draw
him. The dusk had fallen. No sound came from
the niche where the old marshal sat. Frederick
remained where he was; in a lower key, forget-
ful of the failing senses of his friend, he went on:

"I grew old. In the course of time all this
went out of my mind. Who thinks of such
things in his old age? But the outer world
jogged my memory, from time to time. My
beautiful youth outside there — it has been
written and published that he is set up before
my window for his slender limbs to move my
passions. Heavens above! True, it is a beautiful
piece of statuary. Prince Eugene, the old hero,
took pleasure in it, a hundred years ago. Poor
Antinous, so you have to stand there to warm
up my old blood! If they only knew what it is I

117

really look at! Sometimes at the Antinous, yes,
but oftener at the other group, the Flora caressed by Amor. There too is a fine voluptuous
theme: life in full bloom, wooed by the god of
love. But it is not the group I look at. It is the
pedestal. And why at the pedestal? Because
underneath it lies my grave.

"I had it dug out when the terraces were
made. First the grave, then the house. Above
my gable is the name Sans Souci. But it is not
to the house the words refer. It is to the grave.
When I lie there, ah, then I shall be rid of cares
and fears. Then I shall have nothing more to

hide, I shall myself be hidden. No eye shall pierce to where I am. For half a century no man has seen me naked. No servant has quite undressed me, no doctor examined. I have not even seen myself. And when before long I shall stretch myself out in death, in my sleeping-chamber next door, then neither shall they undress me, or wash me, or embalm me. They shall leave me to lie as I am, and cover me with my mantle."

10

FREDERICK had ceased to speak. Out on the terrace nothing moved in the evening air, not a branch, not a tendril. At this very hour, over there in the city of Potsdam, there was bustle and stir; and in Berlin, and Magdeburg, in Cüstrin, in all the fortresses, on all the parade-grounds, in all the cities of the kingdom, in haste, with clamour, the warlike preparations went forward. Mid clatter and clang the army roused itself. The country trembled, its neighbours with it. Here on the height, on the eve of battle, there brooded soundless peace.

From where Lord Marischal sat issued no word, no audible breath. At last the King made up his mind to approach him. It was quite dark in the niche, he could distinguish nothing.

"My lord!" he said, into the stillness. No answer came. He bent, and looked into Keith's face.

Keith was asleep.

The King drew back. But then, almost at the same instant, he smiled. And this was perhaps the sweetest smile of all his life.

He sat down on the tabouret without making a sound and regarded the sleeping man. His eyes grew used to the darkness and he saw.

Peacefully, his head a little bent, the aged man slumbered. Unconsciously Frederick took

off his hat, as though in the presence of death.
Was it death indeed? Was it into the ear of
death he had made his bitter confession?

He could scarcely tell. If it was not today,
not at this moment Keith's life went out, a life
already far fuller of years than is the common
human lot — if it was not today, then it would
be tomorrow, in a few more days, a few more
weeks. How much could he have heard, with
the dull cold ear of age, how much have
grasped of what he had heard? When, at what
point in the painful tale had he fallen asleep?
What could he, whose memory was so short,
recall on waking — if indeed he waked?

"Farewell, my hero," said the King softly,
not unmoved. "Go on before me. Be my quartermaster, order me lodgment in the land of
empty dreams."

Alcmène

1

ON the Ring in Neisse, in front of the old episcopal *Kämmerei,* in the early dawn of a summer day, the suite of princes, generals, and foreign guests stood and waited for the King. At their head, on a beautiful bay horse, sat the Crown Prince, a pleasant-faced gentleman of forty years, already rather stout. Behind him, waiting in a silence that was profound, stood a gay and brilliant host, with a considerable sprinkling among the Prussians of French, English and Russians, Spanish and Dutch. The sensation of the day in Neisse was

that among the foreign officers present at this year's review were two opponents in the American War of Independence: the British General Lord Cornwallis, victor of Camden and Guilford, and the youthful Lafayette, already honoured like a god in his native land. At dinner on the evening before — a meal at which but four courses had been served, washed down by a rather doubtful Bergerac — the two had faced each other across the table: a piquant situation such as could come about only at these extraordinary Silesian reviews. The other guests, quartered about the town, discussed it deep into the night.

But now no one spoke. They had scarcely slept, and besides it was not a moment to be noisy. There was no sound but the occasional ring of a hoof on the uneven pavement. The red light of dawn came up over the house-tops, suffused the ancient market square, and wakened mild answering gleams from costly weapons, gold and silver cordons, and all the highest orders in Europe.

At every window in the low houses round

the Ring people appeared, in night-gowns, in night-caps, in shawls; they leaned over their carven lattices and kept their eyes fixed on the arcades before the narrow, high-gabled *Kämmerei,* and on the white horse with a red saddle that a groom was holding.

The clock in the Kreuzkirche struck two slow, heavy strokes: half past four. The clock on St. James's followed with two more, brisk, clear, and loud; the King stepped out from one of the heavy arches, took off his hat, and quickly put it on again.

A gentle rustle passed over the square as all the gorgeously betrimmed and beplumed head-coverings saluted in response. Everybody held his hat outstretched at arm's length before him, a cloud of powder shook out over the assembly.

Frederick stood beneath the arch, his figure turned slightly away, little and lean in his blue infantry uniform with red facings and collar.

He looked no way different from a subaltern, except for the embroidered star of the Order of the Black Eagle and the rather richer shoulder-cord of silver strands that hung from his right shoulder. It was a new one, by rare exception; it, too, glittered in the sun.

He stood some moments and looked round, with a very bilious, dissatisfied look. His temper, at all the reviews this year, had been atrocious. He spoke to nobody, was frigid to the point of rudeness. The previous evening at table he had shown no courtesy even to Lafayette, and after an uncomfortable hour had disappeared.

"No courier come?" he broke the silence to ask, in that high-pitched, thrilling voice which so often contrasted with the cutting words it uttered. An adjutant came hastily forward and reported. No new courier was come.

Among the suite they exchanged cautious, meaning glances. The Silesian reviews had lasted a week, and every day these mysterious messages had come, awaited and broken open by the King with the last degree of impatience. They had seen the fugitive red rise in his yellow cheek, his hands tremble as they broke the seal and unfolded the paper, and a pantomime of distress and dread pass over his face. Wherever it was, riding, at inspection, during an address, an audience, at table, he forthwith demanded paper and pencil, wrote some lines, sealed them himself with care, and sent the chasseur posting back to Potsdam. The wretched man snatched a hasty meal of sorts, and dashed back hot-foot with the missive through the heavy going of Silesian and Brunswick loam and sand, changing his nag at every post.

What was going on? Everything was possible. The sorry old creature there in the archway was as much the focus of all European eyes as at this moment he was of the international body of generals here assembled. He stood for a power great enough to make him welcome as an ally to any sovereign in Europe; but they found him unfathomable, enigmatic, they shunned him, and Prussia stood for the moment rather lonely in the world. What was on the cards? A new war — though since the War of the Succession the soil of Europe had seemed to be at peace? Or was the bond between Prussia and Russia slipping, the accord between Vienna

and St. Petersburg become a powerful factor?
Was the alliance between Prussia and France,
so long desired, about to be concluded? Had
the matter to do with Frederick's far-reaching
plans for an alliance of German princes? Or
was the Emperor Joseph getting his way after

all, and giving up the Netherlands in order to add Bavaria to his hereditary domains? The grim old man yonder in the blue infantry uniform might at that very moment be holding the fate of Europe in his gouty hands. In his army he had created an instrument of the most formidable striking-power, capable of being the decisive factor in every conflict on the continent. And his martial glory, forged and tempered in battles that today were legendary, would sweep in the van of his army like a scythe.

What was going on? What meant these hurrying posts between Potsdam and Silesia, whose content so obviously moved this most composed of men? The like had never been seen. In their billets, at shaky tables in the houses of magistrates, green-grocers, and parsons, the foreign guests sat every evening after the day's manœuvres, and wrote out in diplomatic French reports to their commanders, their chancellors, their sovereigns. And hardly a capital in Europe but felt a secret tremor whose source was a dispatch from Glogau, from Liegnitz, from Jauer, from Neisse.

132

The King stepped up to his old white horse. As the groom seemed not nimble enough, Lord Cornwallis, in his red general's uniform, sprang down and gave the King his hand to mount. Without looking at him Frederick set his foot in the white-gloved hand. For a moment the Englishman had before his eyes the worn riding-boot, once black, now rusty brown. He felt scarce any weight, so lean and light the old man was.

When he was mounted, and only then, the suite covered. He set his white horse in motion, the gentlemen followed him by twos, slowly; with snorting of horses and clattering of hoofs the cavalcade wound down a narrow street to the river-bank.

2

On the other side one saw the half-erected Friedrichstadt, the creation of the King. But they did not cross the Neisse, they rode along the right bank, through a pleasant landscape, with the river always in sight. The King had set his horse at the gallop almost at once. He loved the easy gait, it was kinder to his old bones.

So he rode along, and all eyes rested on the course, shabby cloth back, above which danced the thin pigtail. Frederick on a horse was not an inspiring sight. He sat abominably and let himself be tossed about anyhow, with dangling legs. There was even contempt in the way he rocking-horsed along in full view of that brilliant and distinguished troop, under the eye of the élite of Europe. Why, thought some among the Prussian gentlemen, must he ride so badly as all that? Many could remember him in earlier years, when he had sat his horse, perhaps not with a faultless seat, but still decently enough,

and taken pleasure in good horse-flesh. Splendid horses were got for him, in England, in Spain, in Barbary itself, and the names of his favourites were well known in the army and among the people—names like trumpet-calls and summons to fiery deeds: Tiger, Springer, Cerberus, Diamond, Star-face, Fury. But all

135

these were dead long since, and it was his next whim to give his horses the names of statesmen: one was called Pitt, one Kaunitz, two others Choiseul and Brühl. But for years now this old white horse had come with him to the manœuvres. Apparently it had no name at all, it sidled along on feeble elderly legs and he quite mildly encouraged it by twitching the reins or clucking — or, when all else failed, tapping it between the ears with a little switch. Spurs he had never worn, and when a chamberlain one day wondered why, Frederick promptly suggested that he bare his own belly and let somebody stick a fork into it. That would give him the information he required.

The foreign guests must have been uncommonly struck with his bad seat when they recalled the occasion of their present ride.

The previous day there had been a so-called grand review. Fifteen battalions of infantry and thirty squadrons of cavalry had deployed in mock battle, a joint display which was to have brought the visit to Neisse to a close. The shift to Breslau was to have taken place today;

there, as always at this time of year, the deco-
rated streets, the provincial authorities, the
Chambers, the citizens, were awaiting their
King. Petitions and memorials were copied out
fair, the refectory of the Rathaus was swept

and garnished for the ceremony of recep-
tion, which, however much of a burden and
vexation of spirit it was to the King, he had
never yet shirked.

Yesterday's review had lasted eight hours. So
much the briefer was the King's criticism. The
infantry and heavy cavalry he dismissed with a

137

few cold formal words. But then he had turned
to the Commander of Hussars and the chiefs of
squadrons, and in ringing tones delivered himself thus: "Messieurs of the Green Regiment
of Hussars! I have never seen the like of this
before. I shall have to see it again. If I had cobblers and tailors for my officers of hussars, the
regiment could not be worse. Why, it has simply
gone to the dogs—no precision, no order, no
cohesion. These chaps all ride like monkeys. I
shall see you tomorrow. Dismissed!"

The young Marquis de Lafayette had heard these terse remarks. He was now riding well forwards in the suite, not far off the King. He looked at the unkempt old man swaying loosely about in his saddle; at the streaked and faded facings of his uniform coat, at the frayed and tarnished silver sash slung round the ascetic hips—and his mettlesome head was full of manifold thoughts. Would Frederick have talked of cobblers and tailors to a regiment of cuirassiers? Hardly; for these were almost entirely composed of Prussian nobility, and this so enlightened, so sceptical, so scoffing monarch was by no means so sceptical, or so enlightened, as to put nobility and burghers on the same footing. He befriended the burgher, but he looked down on him. The officers of the hussar regiments were burghers.

"Free and broad-minded as never a king before," thought Lafayette, "a thinking man, an incorruptible eye—but the son of your father after all, a son of your forefathers, a son of your caste, a son of your century. You too, peerless as you are, have your limitations, and

a smaller man may see them, even I. It is my
age that lets me see them, the forty years fate
set between us. But how strange, the lacks and
limitations of a great man do not cheapen his
greatness, they are what makes us love him.
With reverence and admiration is mingled a
little touch of sympathy, and just the mixture
results in love. I find it glorious that this freest
of all kings cherishes a bias in favour of the
nobility; that he tells his hussars they ride like
monkeys, when the way he sits his own old
beast is nothing less than a disgrace. He is more
than a great king, he is a king who gives you to
think. One can cherish freedom in his heart of
hearts, as I do, and yet have room there for this
despot — for something of a despot he surely is.
And anyhow it is glorious, when all is said, that
I can ride here behind him and look at his
warped old back and quite calmly think all this
about him; and that I am twenty-seven years
old and have already done my bit in the world;
and that I shall yet travel many roads, in Europe and across the sea, when this hero has long
lain in his tomb."

They had ridden rather less than an hour, at
a smart pace, when the King turned into a road
that wound off from the river. Clouds had come
up, the sun was high enough to burn. They
rounded a curve and got a sudden view of the
broad expanse of the drill-ground. In a glare
of light, the Green Regiment stood there at
parade, waiting.

The stately host seemed but a cluster of men,
by contrast with the brown-grey trodden expanse stretching beyond and behind it.

Only from close at hand was there any
beauty in the sight. Drawn up in ten sharp,

clean-cut squadrons, the fourteen hundred hussars held a long front, uniformly mounted on small white Hungarian horses. The word had plainly gone forth for the most painful cleanliness and finish, and certainly half the night had been spent scrubbing. The broad blades of the curving sabres glittered, the exuberant ornamentation of the sabretaches, the lacings of the tight *schoitasch* trousers, the shaft of every boot, the stirrups, the spurs. From each left shoulder hung at the same angle the short brown fur, round each green dolman with its light-coloured buttons and loops the same wide chalk-white girdle was drawn at the same calculated slant. The head-gear was striking. This regiment had retained the black felt busby, a high, brimless Hungarian cylinder trimmed with a banderole, a cloth streamer the colour of the dolman and usually worn round the hat. Today the banderoles were unfurled. Just as the King came in sight with his retinue, a high wind sprang up, it threatened a storm. Round the rigid heads of all these hussars the streamers flapped as in greeting; very wide they were, and so long that they touched and mingled with the horses' flying manes. The officers were stationed at the heads of their squadrons, wearing uniforms on which were repeated in silver the regimental braidings of the troops. They saluted with drawn sabres, the staff trumpeters blew a long two-toned signal, and the commander of the regiment spurred up to the King to make his announcement in due form.

"Yes, yes, I know all that," said Frederick. "You can start in."

But before the nervous gentleman could utter his first command, he heard the King's voice again.

"Roll them up," cried Frederick, and pointed to his own head. The officer did not at once grasp his meaning.

"Roll up those things there, those flapping things! We aren't at a fancy-dress ball, sir!"

The colonel turned his horse front and strained to shout the command above the blustering wind. Simultaneously he took off his own busby, the officers in front of their squadrons did the same, the subalterns and then the troops. Minutes long the whole regiment sat there with bared heads in the saddle. It looked like a prayer before action.

And now began that day to which the stoutest old majors in the regiment, its best-tried sergeants, looked back with quite other tremors than all their memories of Croats and Cossacks had power to stir them with.

The colonel had planned to begin with a sham battle.

"Have them ride," said the King. "Riding is what I want to see."

The wind had risen to a storm. Like a wolf it howled across the parade-ground from one black horizon to the other. Thirty paces behind the King stood the suite. The wind kept up a slight rustling and motion in their ranks. The horses danced with nervousness, their well-combed manes fluttered. Fluttered too the costly hat-plumes, the long strands hanging from the epaulets; the jewelled collars rasped against the cloth of the uniforms, the wide silk of the grand cordons snapped at hips and breast.

144

They rode by platoons: walk, trot, gallop. When a slow trot was about to be shown, the King stopped them. "That's not what I want to see. You might as well dance me a minuet." He rode up and took his stand close to the drilling units, bending on their every motion a sharp and peevish regard.

All at once the rain came down with a rush. He gave the order to stop and put on mantles, in all the squadrons. Hastily they offered him his, a great shapeless piece of cloth lined with wolfskin. He motioned them away, and sat his horse morosely through the downpour, just as he was, with nothing on but his shirt, the yellow waistcoat, and the uniform coat worn thin with age.

He turned round to his suite. They had followed his lead. The Prussian gentlemen could not well do less, the foreigners out of courtesy or bravado did the like, though sick at heart in their full-dress uniforms of fine cloth and silk.

Lafayette was the single exception. When the first big drops fell, he had reached behind him and unstrapped his mantle, a heavy, stout, voluminous garment in which he had already ridden out cloudbursts on the American plains. He turned up the huge coat-collar round his neck and secured it in front. Plainly he did not feel called upon to make heroic gestures in face of a downpour and cut short his life for a whim at the age of seven-and-twenty, with an inflammation of the lungs.

What happened next was striking. Frederick, that is, smiled approval and rode up to Lafayette as though he saw him for the first time. Took off his hat as though the weather were of the best, and said with enchantingly courteous inflection: "My lord Lafayette, I have the honour to wish you a very good day. It pleases me that you have come to see me at my work."

Then he turned to the others, and said, in a curter tone, but still in French: "Gentlemen, wrap up. It is raining."

They took his advice, unfortunately rather late; the obstinate old man, himself still uncovered, turned again to the front, to see his hussars ride.

146

It was unheard of. Not enough that the King criticized each squadron, yes, each single squad. He went on to drill single hussars, calling one after another from the ranks. The colonel stood aside, wiping the sweat with the streaming rain from his face, while the King made each man ride: walk, trot, and gallop, check at full speed and turn. Command after command rang out.

Most of the suite had finally resolved to shelter in a hut not far off, a mere roof it was, resting on five columns. There they dismounted and huddled close, each man outraged or annoyed, amused or reflective, according as his

147

nature was. A few of the Prussian gentlemen stopped with the regiment, with them the particularly well wrapped-up Lafayette.

Not once did he take his eyes from the incredible blue figure on the long-suffering white horse. It seemed to shrink under the downpour, as it were to run together. This King, what had he in his mind? He behaved as though he meant to stick it in this frightful weather until he had put the whole regiment, nay, the whole army, through its paces, man by man. "By the Lord," the Frenchman thought, "what we see here we shall not see again to the end of our days!" He called to mind those tales of Frederick that legendlike ran the round of the terrestrial globe: how on the late afternoon of lost battles he would wilfully remain on the field, riding slowly where belated bullets were singing. A rain like this, thought Lafayette, was a greater peril to the exposed old man than Russian or Croatian bullets. It was borne in upon the young general that never had he approached so near the burden and mystery of greatness as in this rain-drenched, white-haired little man, and

148

his own inflammable heart, beneath the sodden cloak he wore, beat high against his breast.

The storm's first fury had lashed itself out, but now a quiet steady downpour went endlessly on.

They rode. One after another the King took them in hand, these peasants' sons from Silesia and Pomerania and the Mark, even from Hungary, Bohemia, and Poland, for troops from many lands came together in the regiment.

"You let your reins hang out too long when you pace," he said to a wide-nostrilled, red-haired stripling who had been hard at it for ten minutes, and for sheer fright and the noise of the rain was certainly deaf to whatever he might say. "You let the reins lie on your horse's neck, you loll in the saddle like a stuck pig, you flop from one side to the other. The horse doesn't use his rump at all," he turned to the officer, "and he gets all ridden down in front."

At another he screamed, as the wretch rode before him at the double: "You jackass, you haven't the first idea how to ride! You ride

149

with the reins, you stick in your spurs, you
drive your animal wild. You ought to be made
to run the gauntlet, you ought to be put in
irons!" And to the officer: "How can the fellow use his weapon when he has no control of
his horse? If he tries to attack a single enemy,
he will bring his horse on so badly that he will
turn and expose his left side and be hewn down
—you'll be hewn down, you ass, and serve you
right. But I'll be after you"—this addressed
to them all, officers and men alike—"I'll see
to it that there is a change. Cavalry like this I
cannot use against the enemy, with such hussars no king could carry on a war!"

In all their hearts despair had long since
yielded to the profoundest resignation. Thus it
was to be. They were condemned through all
eternity to sit their horses in the streaming rain
and be reviled and tormented by this bowelless
old man. How many hours had it been going
on? Surely for four or five. If only they could
have contrived to hate him! But even this they
were denied. How should they hate him, who
exposed himself more pitilessly than he did

150

them? Ah, he knew right well what he was about! The afflicted officers felt their hearts weighed down with a superstitious conviction that this wilful cruelty had its own good and sufficient ground: precisely with this very regiment, with these very Green Hussars, he must have something most particular up his sleeve! Not one of them would have found it further remarkable if that evening the old man were to put himself at the head of their regiment and no other and ride off eastward with it to conquer the Turks or the Persians. True, there was peace at that moment on earth; yet who knew what plans were hatching in that sallow head? These hurrying messengers that came and went every few hours — what did they mean?

Diagonally across the parade-ground rode one of them at full gallop, straight up to the King. At that moment the rain ceased, the midday sun sent down a flickering ray, the water glistened on cloaks and hats, on harness and weapons, all the little puddles and pools on the drill-ground gleamed like silver. With a clear, exultant trill a pair of birds flew past above their heads.

The rider came nearer, already the chasseur's flat satchel showed at his side. Frederick had sighted him, he rode a few paces forward and drew up where Lafayette sat wrapped in his mantle. The Marquis felt a thrust of pity, crossed by a ray of almost religious awe. The King sat his glossy wet beast, and the bright sun lighted up the wreck he had made of himself. The blue uniform like a dripping rag clung to the crooked form, from the shapeless sodden hat the water ran in streams down a face that showed ill and suffering. But the right hand twitched open and shut with the excess of his impatience. The Marquis glanced toward the shelter. The rest of the suite were just emerging, they all looked curiously across. Lafayette saw amongst the foremost the red general's uniform of his opponent, Lord Cornwallis. For his own part, he would have chosen to withdraw, it seemed more fitting. But Frederick was noticing, he lifted his hat and said in a low voice: *"Restez toujours."*

The chasseur had come up. He reined in his

horse and was about to jump off and salute the King. Frederick checked him, stretched out an imperative hand, and eagerly broke open the dispatch.

Lafayette and another gentleman sprang from their horses and hurried to him. He had swayed so violently in the saddle, it seemed as though he must fall. But he saved himself, drew a deep, whistling breath, and had still strength to pull his horse and himself a little to one side. Lafayette saw him in profile: the mouth open, gasping for breath, the eye rounding as though about to spring from his head. Now the lid closed, and a heavy tear rolled down. The young general felt ashamed to stand so near. He withdrew some paces. Utter silence reigned. The courier sat waiting; motionless in the distance stood the hussar front, behind at the hut the guests were peering across.

At length, after several minutes, the King dismounted. He did it regardless of the figure he cut, simply let himself slide down the dripping-wet flank to the ground.

"Have you a pencil?" he asked the chasseur,

153

in a dull, husky voice. The exhausted man did not understand him or else he had none. The King got what he needed from Lafayette, rested the Marquis's note-book against the red saddle of his own horse, drew off his glove, and wrote. The thin hand shook. Lafayette noticed on it a ring with a very large semi-precious green stone, cut without art and of no great value; he wondered why the King should wear it. It was a Silesian chrysoprase, perpetual emblem of the conquered province. Now Lafayette saw the King's lips move, and he heard a word, a name.

"Alcmène!" said Frederick to himself. "Alcmène, Alcmène!" in accents of deepest grief. The Marquis cast down his eyes. He had not heard. He had not understood, it had no meaning for him. He forbade himself to think of it. He would never mention it. It was already forgotten.

Then he heard himself spoken to, and at once he was present again.

"Sire," he replied, "there are seals in the outer pocket." The King found them, folded his note, and sealed it. His eye fell on the wafer; it did not show the Marquis's arms, but a symbolic figure, a Libertas with flowing hair, in a nimbus. Frederick looked at the young hero and a smile, melancholy and comprehending, visited a moment his wet, sick, suffering face and then withdrew.

"Back to Potsdam," he said to the chasseur. "Make haste. I shall follow on your heels." The chasseur darted away.

Frederick beckoned an adjutant. "I shall break off the march. Make the arrangements in Neisse. But first I will have the officers for criticism."

They approached with all speed, in groups: the colonel, the majors, the cavalry captains, the lieutenants, the cornets — fifty or sixty gentlemen in all. They looked ill-used and felt even worse than they looked. Once again Lafayette thought to withdraw.

"*Restez toujours, monsieur,*" said the King.

As he began his criticism, he tried to give his voice steadiness and ring, but did not succeed past the first sentence or so. Then it weakened, it died almost to a murmur. He was still wringing wet, he could not disguise his shivering, his face looked like a dying man's. Several times he was obviously taken by a wave of strong emotion; he stopped altogether and could go on only after a sudden start and painfully visible effort.

"Messieurs," he began, "again today I was thoroughly dissatisfied with the regiment. I made no secret of my feelings. But now I will scold no more. You know yourselves there must be a change for the better. I will only appeal to your consciences, in a friendly spirit — for surely you could not bear the shame of being cashiered!

"Listen to me — I will tell you some things you have never thought about before. It is wrong to say that the cuirassier is a trooper, and the hussar another trooper, and the only difference is in their uniforms. You believe that, and you act accordingly, but it is not so. Cuirassiers, you see, and other heavy cavalry, must carry weight, they have to exert great force. They take their origin from the old

armoured knights, and they are European. But the light cavalry, that is you hussars, you come from Asia. You entered this continent with the Huns and Sarmatians. The Huns and Sarmatians moved with their whole tribe, and the riders on their swift little horses circled round them in swarms and made a living screen. You take your descent from them. So it must be today. You hussars have to

157

draw a living screen behind which the army can sleep and eat in peace. You cannot be light and mobile enough. Now, if a rider is to be light and mobile he must know how to ride. But the hussars in this regiment cannot ride, and in the first and ninth squadrons neither can the officers. They have shown me a slow trot, but the slow trot has nothing to do with you. The gait for you hussars is the trot and at need the gallop. The hussar must be able to check at full speed, in his tracks, and at the same time execute a given evolution. The horses must be ridden easy on the bit and sensitive to the thigh, so that they can both run swiftly and endure long."

Here the King looked down for some time, as though he had forgotten to go on; but he pulled himself together and spoke again, with an effort.

"It is a shame I should have to say these things to you gentlemen, but I see that my words are needed. The truth is, every single one of you must have genius for your calling. You must be clever and cold-blooded enough to do no more than just badger your enemy for hours; then when the right moment comes, you have to swoop down, and be here, there, everywhere and nowhere, all at once. But you can only do that if you have completely mastered your *métier*. You see what an honourable service is yours. Make yourselves worthy of it, apply yourselves better, so that you will always be able for your duty, and even for more than your duty!"

The gentlemen of the Green Regiment cast stolen glances at each other. They were saved. He spoke mildly to them, yes, he actually spoke as one human being to another.

He steadied his voice to speak again:

"Your service is such that I must demand more of a lieutenant of hussars than from a major in the infantry. Your responsibility is far greater than his, your freedom of action too. Each of you is almost as important as the captain of a battleship. At any moment everything may depend on you alone. It is not so with an infantry major. If he is a stout fellow and stands firm and pushes boldly forward

when he gets the order, you can do with him.
But you . . ."

They could have kissed his hand. He carried
them away, he made up for all they had borne.
But what was the matter? He stammered,
stopped speaking, he swayed and staggered
with his mouth open, his eyes vacant. A lieutenant and Lafayette received him in their
arms.

Again the young general heard whispered
the broken syllables of that classic female
name. He looked cautiously round, as though
he had been charged with a secret to keep for
the King.

3

THE visit to Breslau was cancelled, arrangements set on foot for immediate return. Messengers went speeding over every road of the province.

The King's fainting-fit had been brief. Even in the arms of the two officers he came to himself and glanced shortly round to see if he might not gloss over or conceal his sudden weakness. They all pretended nothing had happened. But it was obvious that he was ill; his eyes wore a hard, feverish glitter, his step wavered, and there were moments when his teeth chattered despite him. He was over seventy years old, weakened and spent with hardship and physical suffering, and had been exposed six hours to the storm. It was hardly less than suicidal.

But he insisted on riding back to Neisse. At one o'clock middle day they had to lift him off his white horse in front of the *Kämmerei*. Within hearing of his suite and the assembled

citizenry he ordered his travelling-coach for
two o'clock, and to prevent any personal con-
struction, he further ordered, standing under
the arcades, still as loud as he could, they
should fetch him the great dispatch-box with
the state papers, which went with him every
journey. He mounted to his quarters.

Immense sensation. They were nonplussed.
All round the Ring stood groups putting two
and two together in whispers. They stood every
side but the south, that they might not be over-
heard from behind the curtained windows of
the *Kämmerei*. The extraordinary event took
precedence of all others, but its mystery remained unsolved.

Above stairs Frederick had received the
chest from the hands of his secretary and closed
the door after him. His work might now begin.

His work consisted in letting himself fall,
just as he was, in his hat and sodden uniform,
into an arm-chair, with his hands hanging
nervelessly down; in staring before him as into
a hopeless void, and saying times out of num-
ber, certainly dozens of times, with his fever-

dry lips, out of his contracted chest: *"Mon dieu, ah mon dieu, ah, ciel, ciel, ah grand dieu!"*

Quite blindly his despair, his dreadful anguish of grief availed itself of this articulate cry, which yet possessed for him no logical meaning. Not for nothing has one a long line of Christian autocrats for ancestors; in moments of violent stress they come to the fore. Once even, he wrung his hands, and again two tears flowed down the cavities of his sallow cheeks.

It was too much. He raised himself and began to move up and down, treading heavily, thrusting with his stick, shaking his head, drawing difficult breaths; he tottered about the ancient room, where dusk had fallen behind the curtains, for the weather had turned again for the worse.

Thus the hour passed. When the King heard it strike two, he unbolted the door to the antechamber and called out they should send up the coachman to him.

Pfundt, the coachman, climbed the stairs, with rather a surly face. His gruff ways and his skill at driving were famous all over Prussia. He always addressed his sovereign in a blustering jargon invented by himself, which he shrewdly knew amused His Majesty a good deal. He was a sharp customer and very stingy, and the cutting-short of the Silesian trip pleased him not at all. Each night's lodging less meant a loss of ten thaler, the tax he levied on those whose houses he chose for the King's quarters, in return for the lavish payment they all received.

"We are taking the road," Frederick said. "On the third day you must be in Potsdam."

"I can just as well be in Potsdam in five minutes," began Pfundt, when a quite short sound of a certain quality from Frederick instructed him. "I will try my best, Your Majesty," he said with humility.

"You'll try? You will pull up in front of my door on the third day, or the fourth will see you carting dirt and stones at Oderbruch. *Marche!*"

Pfundt ran down the steps with his laced hat still in his hand, the demurest of expressions on his face. He could hardly have looked less bumptious — for the moment. But at the bottom he summoned his self-assurance, put on his hat, went out of the door, and mounted his box with vast dignity in full view of the postilions and the thronging populace in the square.

The old-fashioned travelling-coach drew up before the arcades. It was an elongated coach-body, with a great expanse of glass. The space between the front window and the box was unusually large, so was it inside between the front and the back seat. But the wagon withal was built so narrow that in the whole there was room for no more than one person — which was more than enough, since Frederick always travelled alone. The frame was old and poor, the blue satin upholstering worn and faded, the body itself had a curious look, being pear-shaped, running to a point beneath and swelling out above. There was nothing rich or princely about the equipage, but such adjectives might be applied to the team, for Frederick never travelled without ten horses. These

165

ten, harnessed in pairs, the best in the stables of Neisse, were shifting easily in their harness. The four rear ones were driven from the box, then came two pairs, each near one bestridden by a peasant lad in his Sunday best; while on the foremost pair sat postilions in the blue, red, and gold liveries of the King. In front of the whole long-drawn-out cavalcade a chasseur checked his prancing blooded bay horse.

Tension and the buzz of voices filled the Ring. To many it seemed they were about to witness a departure for the seat of war. The foreign officers remembered with a start that in this Silesia almost every grove and every walled-in churchyard were a field of battle; the ear half listened for a distant cannonade.

The departure took place swiftly and silently. Suddenly the King stood there beneath the arches, carrying in plain sight the chest with the state papers. At the same moment the chasseur released his chafing bay and dashed on ahead, in order to gain ten minutes at the first relay.

The King mounted the coach and settled

himself quickly. The on-lookers had silently
bared their heads; he did the same, without a
glance through the windows. He seemed to
know the precise moment to acknowledge their
greetings, and did so while looking fixedly

ahead through the length of his coach. This
rigid compliance with the claims of courtesy
had about it something fearfully impersonal,
it looked really ghastly. That evening by lamp-
light the burghers of Neisse were still trying
to express the feelings that had seized them at
the sight—but they did not manage.

The lackey had closed the coach door and
swung himself up to the seat behind. Pfundt

on his box felt the signal imparted by the shaking of the carriage, the ten horses started up. He skilfully regulated their pull by means of the reins, the cortège increased its pace across the sharp flints of the Ring, rounded a turn, and was off.

Crowds were standing as far as the river. They saw the King, sitting staring inside there, with his hat off. Thus they crossed the bridge. But on the other side, as they passed the last houses of Friedrichstadt, Pfundt's right hand performed a single little movement; as by magic the horses responded, mud and water flew from the wheels, and with snorting and rattling and swaying, at a truly infernal pace, the cavalcade streamed off down the high-road to Brandenburg.

In the town behind it a nervous bustle ensued. Now that the ten-horse train had disappeared, Neisse was nothing but a god-forsaken provincial hole, which everyone forthwith arranged to leave, at latest tomorrow morning. Last letters were engrossed, horses ordered, portmanteaus packed. But at the sign of the

Golden Bell, in Jacobi Street, no more than an hour after Frederick had left, two Spanish officers held a faro bank; the ante-room of the lucky landlord was crowded with uniforms, and across the baize-covered table where dignitaries had sat, there streamed a golden flood of imperials, guineas, and ducats. As by common consent they were making up for lost time, directly he had gone, this alarming King who despised all elegant pleasures, to whom play was a pernicious folly, the noble hunt a barbaric horror, and over the threshold of whose villa in Potsdam no woman had stepped a foot these forty years and more. — Among the foreign officers next day were many who could only set out accompanied by serious financial cares.

169

Lafayette was no longer in the town. He had quitted it at once after the King. And while Frederick rattled westward on the Schweidnitz road, he took the highway toward the sunrise, alone and unhurried, behind him with a led horse his groom, an Auvergnois like himself.

He could not have spent another evening in that noisy international crowd, listening to political gossip in mangled French and being plied himself with questions. A strong and silent impulse had been imparted to his spirit today, and he found it good to ride alone and think about the King.

The breast of the young Marquis Lafayette was full of the courage that is born of freedom, of high-hearted youthful emotions that were essentially simple, essentially French. For his mind, it had been nourished on Parisian social theory. A new era was about to dawn; and in his dauntless, clear-eyed faith in humanity he stood in the van to hail it. Over there in the virgin land beyond the sea only the human being counted; and soon in Europe too kings would cease to count. What an exquisite dispensation then, that it had been vouchsafed him to see at such close range the greatest among them, who would certainly have closed his eyes in death before the hour struck for his like! His like? His like did not exist. Truly the old order came to its end here in a most amazing figure! It seemed to the general that he had learned today more and profounder things about the King than any of his contemporaries knew. These perceptions of his were vague and equivocal — and it was just that which gave them the fantastic dimensions of objects seen by a failing light.

He was riding toward the Polish frontier. He had a desire to see the kingdom which the self-interest of the great powers had cut up and partitioned a decade ago. He might get as far as Warsaw, perhaps. It was by no means certain. He came as any other traveller might, without evidence of his rank, wrapped in his traveller's cloak. He had not even a passport. But perhaps they would recognize him — his portrait hung on many a wall in town and village, just as did the King's; and surely not less in the towns and villages of a kingdom conquered and oppressed.

It was a thought to gladden a heart of seven-and-twenty years, and a French heart at that! In the gathering dusk he smiled a little to himself and rode on with steady pace upon his simple, valiant, glorious way.

4

THE mud of the high-road splashed up to the carriage roof. Frederick rocked upon his draggled cushions. He felt anything but good. There was a bitter taste in his mouth, his pulses raced, he alternately shivered and glowed, and ominous pains ran up and down his limbs.

The scene was dreary. Always in other years he had found this Silesia a rich, rewarding sight, compared with his old-Prussian domains: first the goal and then the prize, the pride and preoccupation of his life, the precious province, whose symbol he wore on his right hand. Alas, on this dull afternoon it looked merely dismal, not worth a second glance. Its straggling villages and settlements were more presentable and better built than those in the Mark, but they only excited his disgust. They crawled on and on—as though one were passing an endless string of entrails, he thought. But self-critical still, despite the heaviness of his fever, he was aware that the figure arose from the disorders of his own abdomen, and he laughed harshly all to himself in his glazed cell.

Fresh horses mustered by the chasseur stood ready at each relay station, mounted by peasants' sons, who had hastily donned their best

clothes. The unharnessing went forward at top speed. People poured pails of water over the hissing-hot wheels, it made the only sound there was. Everybody looked at the sickly sallow profile in the coach, the almost unbroken straight line of brow to nose, the lower half of the face cut away at a sharp angle. And at the

174

moment of driving off from each station the
King performed the same stiff salute, taking
off his hat without turning his head to look. It
was hardly even a gesture any more, only the
memory of a gesture, as the vehemence of the
fresh team bore him away more madly than
ever.

To right and left lay the historic ground of
his career. Here it was he had sustained those
incredible, now legendary struggles against a
continent, dogged all the time so close by
wretchedness and ignominy that the thought
of death became his dear and friendly refuge.
All about lay the vast graveyard where his
Prussians and his mercenaries, and his enemies
with their mercenaries, lay in their thousands,
coffinless, long rotted, a skeleton army in
mouldy rags of leather and uniform-cloth.
Each year when he passed this way, such
thoughts rose in him and would not be denied.
He thought of his dead friends, his generals
and colonels, for many of whom he had felt affection — they too lay hereabouts, immured in
some corner of some country churchyard. He

175

would call up their faces and their deeds, and think of lofty phrases with which to honour their memory in the annals of his campaigns. Sometimes as he pursued his lonely way he would feel a sort of ironic sympathy for these heroes, and question their shadows to right and left, whether the phantom we call honour, whether five lines in a history-book, could requite them for the untimely death they had died. Unaccountably easy, terribly easy, was it made for princes to carry on their wars!

176

But today nothing of that. No glance, no irony, no coining of phrases, nor pensive memories. The wastes of Siberia could not have passed more unregarded by. He was in a fever, his one thought was to get forwards. At what a snail's pace they drove! The human race, in all the thousands of years of its history, might have discovered swifter means of locomotion. It was too stupid to think of anything. With horses in Darius's time, with horses in Frederick's.

Out of sheer impatience he lost sight over long stretches of the reason for his haste. Then suddenly he would remember, would know to what sad goal he so stormily pressed on. And a stab of pain would go through his breast.

It drew on towards evening, Pfundt would have stopped before now, but got directions to the contrary, and they rattled frantically into hilly Schweidnitz, where lights already burned. This was the fortress that had held out the four famous sieges in the great war; Frederick gave them not a thought, he was already past it and out on the high-road once more. The coach lanterns were lit, two on the box, two more at the corners of the body. The lights flashed on the walls of village after village; windows were flung wide and all eyes stared affrighted at the apparition as it swept thundering past.

When they halted at last, it was quite dark. They were in the province of Hohenfriedeberg and Bunzelwitz. Frederick knew every stick and stone for miles round. In the small village of Polsnitz, at Parson Andreas Künnemann's, he spent a bad, an almost sleepless night.

Off again at early dawn. Rapid changing of horses at stations, water hissing over red-hot wheels; ringing of bells, baring of heads, peasants staring after the train.

On, on, on. Soft and soundlessly through heavy loam, grinding harshly through foot-deep sand, bumping and jolting over stones flung down to mend the road. Hot sun in the early morning. Magnificent summer weather.

Frederick felt much worse today, he wished for the subdued grey light of the day before. Everything hurt him: his eyes smarted with the glaring light, the heat prickled his skin, tender from the perspiration of the night before. He began to cough. His abdomen was hard and distended. He would reach for a pinch of snuff, then drop it again, disgusted by the mere foretaste of the sensation. He hated having people look at him, and stared straight ahead; when a hesitating cheer arose, his nausea redoubled.

Field of battle far and wide, land of heroes, land of glory, land of tombs. He passed without a glance. The sun was in the west when they neared the town of Sagan, and he ordered them to make a detour round it. Pfundt made a face, pulled furiously at the reins, and would have turned leftward to Sorau. Frederick pounded on the pane with his stick and motioned in the other direction. "Ass," he muttered. "They are all asses." Pfundt had to go back over the Bober—the King, in all his preoccupation, had borne in mind that the road was better on the right bank. They neared the borders of the Mark.

He felt very bad. More and more the fever took hold on his blood and brain, at moments

179

his consciousness grew blurred. They had just
changed horses, in a place called Naumberg,
when there happened a peculiar thing.

The sun was already low, and struck the
King in his aching eyes. He took off his old
uniform-hat, which he had been wearing in mil-

itary fashion, with the point in front. He undid
the tarnished cord and let down the black flap,
intending to put it on the other way round, to
protect his eyes. He held it so in his hand.

A few days ago he had been travelling eastward to the Silesian manœuvres, the morning
sun had hurt his eyes and he had let down the
flap. Now he was travelling westwards, and
letting down the flap in the afternoon. Thus
it was now, thus had it been the year before,
thus it had always been. Always on the fifteenth of August he left for Silesia, and the
sun burned his face in the forenoon; and he
held the manœuvres in Silesia and travelled
back, and the sun burned his face in the afternoon.

The circumstance, in his fevered brain, took
on mighty dimensions. He saw himself as an
old marionette, for ever going through the
same motions. In the beginning he had always
had to make war, regardless of all the beautiful
bright things of life — literature and music,
and pleasant converse with lively minds. He
had had to keep moving about, carrying on

wars, living within smell of powder and dead bodies, and getting old and ugly doing it. Then home again, used up, cheerless. His friends died away, all literature turned for him to empty husks, its charm departed; his flute he could no longer hold for gout. The year became a rigid, corpse-like round of affairs and duties. There was the long, frightful winter to be got through, and when that was done, the reviewing began. Review on the fourth of May in Charlottenburg, review on the seventeenth of May in Potsdam, on the twentieth in Berlin, the twenty-sixth in Magdeburg. Review on the second of June in Cüstrin, on the fourth in Stargard, on the eighth, ninth, and tenth of June in other out-of-the-way places. Then on June the twelfth he received the Finance Minister, and the budget was made up for the year, item by item. That went on weeks and months, and then on the fifteenth of August came the journey to Silesia, and the sun burned his face in the forenoon on the way thither, and in the afternoon on the way back, and he turned his hat round this way and that — just a puppet,

drawn by cords like those that danced up and down on his hat, a melancholy old ghost. . . .

He clutched suddenly at his forehead, he pulled himself together. What was the matter with him, what was he doing? Actually he had been illustrating the dreary jog-trot of his thoughts by taking off and putting on his old hat, first one way and then the other, mechanically, rapidly, without a sound. His brain was still going round.

It was the fever. He was seriously ill. It must be brought under control without loss of time. A good dose of quinine would do his business.

Evening had come round again. In the falling darkness they drove into the little town of Crossen, at the point where the Bober flows into the Oder.

Light showed at a window on the ground floor of a dignified house on the market square. A magic light it was, issuing from a pot-bellied vessel filled with pale-green fluid, with a taper burning behind it. This was the apothecary's shop.

Frederick had in mind to get out, to enter the shop and take the drug as he stood. But his legs went back on him. He had to be lifted down. He decided to stop the night. Was not every house in Prussia his house?

184

5

A FIGURE carrying a lighted taper entered the dark and spacious entrance hall from the first door on the right: a tall, broad man, already grey-haired, with an open, tranquil gaze: Henschke the apothecary. He recognized the King, and made a suitable inclination of his body, yet without betraying any confusion or undue obsequiousness. Frederick felt relieved; his nerves were already too much on edge to bear the thought of going through with unnecessary formalities. He was taken with the apothecary at once, and asked graciously:

"I suppose I can stop the night here? But you'll have to be my doctor too."

The room into which the King was ushered was both laboratory and salesroom; fitted out with cupboards and presses, distilling-apparatus, retorts and weighing-machines, a retreat worthy of an alchemist.

At once he asked for his quinine bark. The chemist glanced at his face, listened to his

185

cough, and set to work to triturate the drug for use.

"Your Majesty has fever," he said as he worked, in his quiet way. "And quinine will help the fever, but the fever is not the illness."

"You're not a doctor, are you?"

"Your Majesty, I have served two campaigns as company surgeon. But not much knowledge is needed to see that Your Majesty has a cold on the chest. And probably the bowel is affected as well."

"Quite right, it is. But what will you do for it?"

"I should suggest some of the new powder used by Dr. Kurella of Berlin. It will help the fever, and also act as a mild purge."

"What is it made of? I've no great confidence in any of those infernal drugs."

"Fennel, Your Majesty; senna, licorice, sugar, and sulphur."

"Sulphur, eh? Didn't I say it was infernal? Well, give it me, anyhow."

"It should not be taken at once after the quinine. Your Majesty should take it in a half-hour or so, perhaps after Your Majesty is in bed."

"Where can I sleep?" asked the King. He felt very ailing, and inclined to yield to these gentle, explicit ministrations. The apothecary opened the next room, where a wide double bed was visible. Henschke was a widower, and slept here below to be on hand for night calls.

"Just today it was made up fresh," he said, unembarrassed. "Shall I call the servant to undress Your Majesty?"

"I'll undress myself," the King said, though he could barely stand. "Then come in to me with the powder."

"If Your Majesty were so gracious as to pardon a suggestion — it would do Your Majesty so much good to have a wet pack all over."

"Not the slightest use," said Frederick, ungracious on the instant. "I'm no infant. Go on out now."

Henschke closed the door after him, crossed the unlighted laboratory, and sat down in a chair by the window, as far away from the bedchamber as possible.

187

He looked through the clear green light out into the market-place, where the travelling-coach still stood before the door. The horses had been taken out, and it was surrounded by half the population of the place. Sometimes a figure would come close and peer into the narrow interior, at the worn blue cushions, awe and embarrassment in his face.

The chemist's tranquil bearing was not assumed. He had a stout, honest heart in his breast, and besides he was too old to have many wants or wishes left. This was not the first time in his life he had seen the King. He sat at his magic window and thought how wretched the old man looked today — as though already marked down for death. And what a will! His doctors must have a hard time with him. He had been friendly at first, then afterwards how gruffly he had repulsed the idea of the cold pack, which would have been so good for him! Henschke recalled the current gossip about the King — that he was not formed like other people, and was afraid to expose his body. It was said that not even a valet had ever seen him naked. Some folk professed to know that he had a great flaming red mark, the devil's sign manual, across his breast, which was soft and like a woman's in shape. The apothecary smiled sympathetically, in his magic twilight. What poor powers of invention that showed — a soft white maidenly bosom beneath the tobacco-stained yellow waistcoat! As though such childish fables could add any touch of the miraculous to the figure of this old man!

But the time was up; he went back into the sleeping-chamber.

The King lay in bed, hardly undressed at all. He was having chills. His cough shook him. The chemist administered the powder.

"You think that will help me?"

"It is a capital remedy. But Your Majesty could help it work by lying closely covered with feather-beds, and drinking hot tea, to induce a perspiration."

"That's right. You know your trade."

"Oh, Your Majesty, it is simplicity itself. Any village barber should know that much — and they do."

"All the same, you're a clever fellow. I'm glad I fell into your hands."

Henschke went and brought the tea. The King began to catechize him. Such was his habit, for fifty years back.

"Children?"

"One son, Your Majesty."

"Why not more?"

"My wife died soon after his birth."

"H'm. Puerperal fever?"

"Yes, Your Majesty, puerperal fever."

"No remedy for that in your shop?"

"There is none, as yet. It is a puzzling contagion. The midwife probably carries it from house to house without knowing it. In the great lying-in establishments in Paris women die of it by the dozen in a single day."

"Horrible," said Frederick. "Doctors still know much too little. Die, die, die," muttered he to himself, in a singsong tone, that rang with fever. And at this thought of death a look of grief passed over his face that had little to do with any young women in the hospitals of Paris. But he recovered himself. His head was

190

sunk deep in the pillows but he turned it round
on Henschke and went on with his cross-exami-
nation:

"You say you served as surgeon in two campaigns? Where was that?"

"In the great war with the Margrave Karl's
regiment; in the last war with von Pirch, in the
army of Prince Heinrich."

The King knitted his brows. He did not love
to be reminded of this last campaign of his old
age, which had been as disastrous as it was victorious. And he did not care either to be re-

minded of his brother Heinrich, with whom he
had definitely broken.

"Well, you hadn't many wounds to bandage
there."

"No, Your Majesty, but the more sick to
nurse."

"What made you go, anyhow? You were no
longer young by then."

Henschke was silent. He got red.

"You needn't be afraid to tell me."

"Decent medical officers are badly needed in
Your Majesty's armies."

"Right, again. In all my wars my orders were
carried out as badly as possible. Nothing has
vexed me more. Often they have treated my
poor men barbarously."

It was seldom Frederick's way to discuss his
thoughts and purposes with inferiors. But he
fancied this apothecary. And his inner man felt
oddly shaken up—not the fever alone was the
cause.

"But I have given such orders now," he said,
"as will put the rascals and do-nothings out of
the business."

192

"I am afraid," said Henschke, "that Your Majesty is very far from knowing all."

"Why do you say that?" Frederick asked eagerly, in some irritation. "What makes you think so?"

"From my own observation, and from a learned physician, formerly head surgeon in von Pirch's regiment."

"What is his name?"

"Dr. Rutze, of Stettin."

"You can write it down for me afterwards. And now say plainly what you have to say, don't mince matters. The war is not so long over. The guilty are still alive, they can be punished. Things must improve. Yes, it was awful, awful," he said again, softly, and seemed to be rapt in another vision of death.

The sweat induced by the medicament began to run down his jaded limbs. He was most uncomfortable, even suffering; he had pains in the bowel, which had not yet yielded to the treatment, his heart beat oppressively. He was in fit state to receive upon his nervous system the full force of the horrible tale he was to hear.

193

"Now," said Frederick. "No quibbling. Out with it."

Henschke still did not speak. From a medical point of view, it was certainly not right to occupy a sick man's mind with such horrible facts. Yet it was his duty. This moment had come like a gift from heaven, it would never come again, and much good might flow from it. And this old man obviously set no further store by his own life, the only thing he still cared about was to be Providence and servant to his people; and, even in his fever, even in his suffering, he had a right not to be spared. Henschke felt a wave of emotion go through him; his calmness gave way to a thought like a flame; yes, what he had before him was heroism, the height of the human spirit; here it lay, encased in that pitiable little frame, that perishable, unpretentious husk. He said to himself: "This is the climax of my life, my great moment is at hand. I feel it. I shall never feel it again. I cannot prolong it. This old, ailing man, the King of kings, the first among men, he lies here before me and gives ear to his people."

All that passed through him quickly. Then he spoke. He told his story.

In the last campaign, in the War of the Bavarian Succession, hardly a shot had been fired, yet a good part of the army had fallen. Malignant fever had raged, as it had before in the Seven Years' War; they called it putrid, or bilious fever, and they were powerless against it. But even worse had been the dysentery. The treatment for this tormenting and repulsive ailment might of itself be called simple enough: the patient must lie well covered in bed, be given light diet, such as broths. milk, and gruel, and have warm poultices applied to relieve the severe pain. But the most elementary necessities were wanting, or, if not wanted, wasted in the most careless or criminal way; stolen, or intercepted, while hundreds and thousands of sufferers, weak unto death, had to eat army bread. The best they got was a soup that tasted like ditch-water, with a few kernels of barley, half-cooked or maggoty meat, turnips, potatoes, and cattle-beans. Large sums, of course, were set down in the books for good, nourishing

sick-diet. But the regimental surgeons and or-
derlies caroused on the wine; and sold to the
highest bidder the rice, white flour, and finer
vegetables, as well as the vinegar and drugs.
The care of the sick was in the hands of impossible persons, and this in itself was the source of
all the evil. The sick-orderlies were hard-shell
old non-commissioned officers, who knew as
much about sick-nursing as they did about
water-colour painting, and had grown callous
with long years of routine. The field-doctors
and company surgeons were as ignorant as
bone-setters, in fact they were mostly bone-
setters, a rough and ignorant crew, hardly capable of the most elementary first aid; and there
were far too few of them, often but one to two

196

or three hundred sick. Higher-class physicians there were who followed the regiment, often serious men with scientific training. But they could not give personal attention to all these hordes of sick. And even among them were rascals enough, who gambled away in the officers' casino money entrusted to them for medical supplies. Some of them were too nervously organized, too fastidious, to go to work energetically; they contented themselves with issuing general orders and giving a glance in the halls where the sick were—and, as Henschke admitted, you could scarcely blame a man of any refinement for that.

For these halls were simply hell. A bed was never seen. The sick lay on straw, in rare cases on a mattress, many quite simply on the floor. Covers there were none. Men in high fever lay with nothing over them but their soldiers' cloaks, stiff with a hundred pelting rains. Everything was alive with bugs, black-beetles and lice. But this was not the worst. There were as good as no night-stools, the privies were few, and too far off for many of the sick to have

197

strength to reach them; so the floor lay full of
blood-impregnated and infectious excrement.
Often there was literally not a clean spot to set
one's foot on. There was never any fumigation,
seldom a window opened, no servant could be
found to clean out these human stables. A
frightful atmosphere reigned, as in a slaughter-
house at high summer, a pestilential stench of
sewer and grave. Anyone who came here sick
might give up hope, he could feel himself rot
while he still breathed. And if anyone did leave
these infernal regions alive, to be sent farther

down the line, he had still the worst before him. For the ambulances made not the smallest provision for racked and shattered bodies. Most of them were simply requisitioned farm-wagons, on which the men were flung like calves. Covers or pillows were unknown, and so they were driven, through cold and storm. Every jolt, every turn of the wheels was martyrdom to the sufferer, until he fell into a merciful faint. If any died, they were thrown down off the wagon —sometimes, by mistake, one might be thrown down living, to die altogether in the mud.

The apothecary had told his tale. He had not dared look at the King while he spoke. Now, in conclusion, he said: "Surely it must seem presumption in me, a medical understrapper and provincial subject, to say things which are plainer to the all-seeing eye of Your Majesty than they are to me. But Your Majesty knows the thing in general, and the sum total; what I had before my eyes was a section of misery small enough for me to grasp, as a sovereign can seldom get to see it. Furthermore, the sectors Your Majesty saw were naturally much better than the others, since they would have taken care not to steal or shirk or be cruel to the sick when Your Majesty was by."

The King had been lying with his eyes shut. He opened them now. His first words were: "Have you a pencil? Write down for me the whole name and address of your Doctor Rutze."

Henschke wrote. Then at the King's order he took the blue uniform coat off the chair where it lay across the box with the state papers, and put away the address in an inner pocket.

Much that was new the King had not heard. As Henschke naïvely put it, he knew the thing in general and the sum total; the individual misery had as far as possible been kept from him. Ah, yes, he could not be everywhere, he had to delegate power and show confidence even where he had none. This honest apothecary did not dream how doggedly the King was labouring at the improvement of the sanitary administration, with what grim concentration on detail; how anxiously he was bent on bringing about reforms before he went hence.

He was painfully conscious of the sacrifices his wars had entailed. The nobility, the bureaucracy, the upper classes of his kingdom often levelled at him the reproach that he favoured the common man, even beyond the bounds of justice. But who was it he favoured in these peasants and small citizens? Not themselves; no, but the brothers, the cousins and fathers of these, the victims shot down in his earlier wars and mown down by sickness in his last one.

He had never quite succeeded in bringing it to bay, that secret instinct that had driven him on to the heavy deeds for which he stood re-

201

sponsible. Never had he quite drawn the black veil from its face. He had been swept away on his life's course, he had fought and stood fast; the world was his witness that he had accomplished the extraordinary; he had suffered thousands and tens of thousands to be shot down, to rot in stinking holes, wretchedly tended by scoundrelly knaves — he had known all that and been helpless to mend it. But at least he could swear that he had shared their lot, of his own free will; it had come naturally to him to risk death as they did, to have no better bed, no better food, certainly no better sky above him, or even, if possible, a worse one.

What did it matter? It would soon be over now, his time was at hand. The one thing he still had, the only thing he still could love, that too was now taken from him: something precious and tender, for which one could feel a pure and guileless grief, as one could not for those Bohemian and Sorbian peasants dead of dysentery. "Soon," he thought, "soon I shall lie down in our common grave, that is already dug, and sleep away war and misery and wrong done and suffered, sleep away fame and hatred, and all the tumult of this world. I am worn out, I am ripe for death, this fever and illness are the beginning of my end. Oh, welcome, welcome death! I have lived my life."

He roused himself with a start. "So he knows, does he, your Rutze?" said he, as though his thoughts had been all the time on the physician.

"Assuredly, Your Majesty. As regimental surgeon he saw much, improved what he could, and spoke out regardless. He knows more than anyone else about the rascality that went on, and no one hates it so much."

"I've never heard of him."

"Because he made enemies among the corps doctors and the authorities. They were to blame for his resignation, too."

"I'll write to him."

There was a pause. The King gave a little groan. Then he seemed to think of something. He wrinkled his brow, and said grumpily:

"What about you? Don't you want anything out of me?"

Henschke blushed — either for himself, or for the King, or for the race of men with whom His Majesty had had experience.

"Your Majesty, I am quite content."

"Ah, very good," said Frederick. "Then let me get some sleep."

But Henschke asked leave to sit up in the room; and since the King had just urged him to express a wish, and was moreover feeling far from good and lacked his usual servant, the request was granted.

Profound stillness reigned. A tiny oil light burned. At times it flickered and seemed on the point of going out. Then the hollows in the face of the King became black pits, and Henschke saw his death-mask. This great light among lights, it too was flickering; and it was his, Henschke's, privilege to hold his bleached and puckered apothecary-hands about it and guard it for a night. It gave him a feeling of consecration.

But there was not much to do. A few times he gave the King to drink, and he was permitted to wipe the streaming perspiration from

the face and wash it off with lukewarm water.
Once the King sent him from the room. The
sick man slept a good deal, but never long together, for he started up often as in fright. He
talked loud in his sleep and uttered names,
some of which were known to the apothecary,
for they belonged to the history of the time.
Several times Rutze was mentioned, Frederick
seemed to be in talk with him, to question him
impatiently; he would say sharply: "What's
that, what's that?" and give a murmur of satisfaction at the reply. Then it would seem some

painful impression forced its way into his mind. "I can't put my foot down anywhere," he complained, and Henschke saw his feet move under the covers as though feeling about. "That is not so, Rutze," he cried out again, after a while, in strong excitement; "Rutze, Rutze, listen, let me tell you!" The apothecary began to understand. The King was defending himself against the vile assertion that went the rounds during the Seven Years' War in the outside world and even in Prussia: to the effect that the King ordered his doctors to pay no further attention to crippled or useless soldiers, but to let them die and save their keep. *"Ce n'est pas vrai,"* cried Frederick, tossing about in the bed. "Rutze, *ne le croyez pas. On m'a calomnié."*

Tears came in Henschke's eyes. Then he saw that the King had roused. He groaned softly, perhaps he thought himself alone.

"How does Your Majesty feel now?" asked the apothecary.

"Ah, my dear Henschke," replied the King, in a weak, low-spirited voice. "How should I feel? I am only an old bag of bones, good for nothing but to be turned out to pasture."

Henschke was deeply shocked. "Have I a right to be hearing such dreadful words?" he thought. But the King had dropped off again. It wore on toward morning.

His fancies took a pleasanter turn, and more peaceful. He seemed to be playing, coaxing someone. "Come here, come here!" he called out several times quite loud and clear, smiled as though pleased, and moved the fingers of his right hand beneath the sheet. Was he calling a dog? Yes, he not only called, he entered into conversation, in which he took both sides and made barking noises in response to his own teasing; "Bow wow wow," said he, and smiled a gentle, friendly smile.

By daylight he lay in deep sleep. He had left no orders to be waked, so the apothecary saw to it that perfect quiet reigned in the house, wrapped the knocker of his shop, and stationed a watch outside to make passers-by keep a wide berth.

At eleven the King waked, distinctly better, but furiously angry at the lateness of the hour.

207

Henschke would have explained, but got a snub for his pains. Tired with his night of watching, he submitted. The King wrote out an order for a hundred thaler in payment for his lodging, handed it to him as cool as you please, settled himself in his coach, and drove off.

6

Oatfields, fir-trees, still-flowing streams, sometimes a pond, dignified with the name of lake. His native land was assuredly the most tedious scene beneath the sun. The only bright spots were the peasant women on the way, in their black stays, black head-cloths, and short, staring red frieze skirts. It was the Wendish costume. This ancestral province of his, the Mark of Brandenburg, was actually not occupied by Germans, but by Slavs, Eastern peoples, even Asiatics. You saw it by the cheek-bones, by the compressed and slanting eyes. And you had only to hear the place-names for miles round: Baruth, Goyatz, Cottbus, Schwiebus, Lebus, Podelzig, Polenzig, Peitz. Potsdam, even, sounded anything but German. Yet there was all this rubbishing talk about a nation, and he himself was a national hero, save the mark! People believe anything you tell them. There was the much-trumpeted national unity of the French, for instance. Yet in Paris a cou-

ple of hundred years ago more Flemish —
which meant more German — was spoken than
French. But the fact was, a people were easier
to lead if they could think of themselves as a
whole, and a very select whole at that. His
Wendish-Sorbian subjects considered themselves quite a choice and superior kind of Germans, though the land they dwelt in was the
drearest on the face of the globe.

With a sudden stab came back that thought
— he had not had it now for some time: his
whole life had been spent in these unblest regions, his life that was now closing. Could it be
true? Had he never drawn breath save heavily
under these heavy skies, with their driving
clouds? Never felt a southern sun, or seen a
blue sea, nor a grove of stone pines, nor a palm?
No, nothing. All that he knew of the hot countries was the pair of apes that had torn his win-
dow-curtains, and an Arabian dromedary, used
to transport his snuff-boxes when he moved for
the winter weeks from Potsdam to Berlin. Yes,
they summed up his knowledge of the Orient
and the South.

But he had seen nothing of Europe either.
As a young man he had once been in Strass-
burg, and once in Holland. That was an end of
it. Paris, his spiritual home, the home of all pure
and elegant culture, Paris, that he loved, he had
never seen. He had never seen Italy, the temples and statues of antiquity, never stood where
his prototypes, Hadrian and Marcus Aurelius,
had spent their days. He had never even visited
Vienna, nor did he now, though a visit was long
overdue to the Kaiser, his political enemy and
personal admirer. He had gone from one dirty
village to another, and carried on war, and between times sat at his sloping desk. He had to
work, day in, day out, year in, year out, from
three in the morning up to nightfall and beyond. He had to work for men he despised, and
saw nothing of the gay, beautiful, manifold
countries of the earth, though they rang with
his glory in a hundred tongues.

Glory? Was it fame that made up to him for
all that he lost? In youth, at one time, he had
thought it would. But when it came, when he
possessed it, it was a laughing-stock. What sort

of goal was that, to bulk large in the minds of such a pitiful race; what a kingly ambition, to want to keep on parading like a ghost through the heads of their children's children, who would not be a whit less rude or stupid than they were themselves!

Or perhaps he had been working for the happiness of mankind, to save them pain, to create

212

better and more beautiful living-conditions for them? Even to this day was that not the goal of all his efforts?

They were driving through Beeskow, and involuntarily he gazed northward in the direction of Frankfurt. Up there lay the Oderbruch, a province he had reclaimed and populated, at great personal sacrifice. A whole new province it was, won by peaceful means, and once he had taken pride in the act of creation. Today he felt like asking himself if it was any better off now than when it was inhabited by wildfowl and reptiles. Was it ever possible to create or to increase the sum of happiness? It was highly probable that his colonists dragged their wives about by the hair and regaled their children with kicks.

Did he at least get thanks for his pains, was he beloved in his land? He did not believe so. An episode of the late war crossed his mind — he often thought of it in his bad days. In camp at Burkersdorf a large consignment of forage had been lost to the enemy by his own fault, through some oversight in his orders. When the

213

fact was known, there was general glee. He
happened to overhear a group of officers making jokes about him and slapping their thighs.
He had drawn back, said nothing, punished nobody. He had been ashamed. It was not among
the vulgar that the thing had happened, but in
his army, among his officers, his aristocracy. He
had lived too long, he was a burden, they were
like servants relieving their minds in private
about the master. It was his fault, he was often
severe, his punishments often degrading; he
had inherited more of his father than he real-
ized when he was young. And he paid for it, ah,
yes, he paid dear. He was unloved.

A hand clutched at his heart. He was hasten-
ing to that which had loved him, to that which
he had loved. With burning eyes he stared
through his front window, past Pfundt's broad
back, westward. They had passed Grossbeeren,
and it was already dark again.

The horses snorted, the wheels ground
through the sand, they whirled madly on. There
at last were the familiar lanterns of the last village, before the pastor's house and the pot-

house door. It was a dark still night, the wind was down, the air mild, as the ten-horse team drew near Sans Souci from the back, up the winding drive. The villa was lighted up.

Now people came running down the slope — Schöning, Neumann, and Strützky, with cressets in their hands. With stamping of hoofs and rattling of harness the cortège mounted the easy slope to the back entrance, accompanied by the servants.

The King let no one help him. The coach had scarcely stopped before he was in the vestibule; he turned straight to the left and strode as fast as his legs would let him through the little gallery, thumping heavily with his cane, holding his strong-box under his other arm. In the short narrow entry that led from the gallery he paused and panted—it was half a gasp of anguish. He hesitated another instant, then pushed open the door and stood in the last room of his suite, the library.

He saw it at once. They had put it on a little low table in front of the chimney-piece.

7

ALCMÈNE, the dog, the Italian greyhound, his darling, his favourite, his only joy—she lay stretched out in death on the little table, covered by a tall shining bell-glass that belonged to a costly clock. There she lay, irradiated by two five-branched candelabra standing on either side of the chimney-piece, their flames repeated in the mirror. She rested on her side as though she slept, her delicate head turned toward the room; the eyelid had lifted slightly, and one caught a glimpse of the dark iris. The spirit-fine little legs lay neatly together, one of the forelegs bent slightly, daintily. The light skin shimmered and gave out silken gleams in the warm candlelight. At first there was no sadness in the sight, it was too hard to believe that this was death; he could hardly resist calling: "Alcmène, Alcmène!" to see her spring upon her little legs.

And yet Alcmène had lain already in the grave.

When Frederick left for the review, she was ailing. He had hardly been able to make up his mind to go. But he was ashamed to leave his work, his army, a whole province, in the lurch, all on account of a dog. At the same time, he was ashamed of being ashamed. Anyhow, he had left, punctually on August fifteenth, as he did every year. The three *Kammerhussars* had orders to send off detailed news of the favourite, every morning. And every evening a jaded officer of the regiment of chasseurs had delivered the two-days-old message into the King's hand. They did not know what it was they carried, for Neumann, Strützky, and Schöning kept their own counsel, not even laughing among themselves, and nursing Alcmène with care and pains — and at length with despair.

It had been of no avail, the delicate creature had died despite them, and they buried her in front of the King's window, near the pedestal of Flora's statue, where several more of his dogs already lay. In fear and trembling they sent on the news.

Yesterday evening the order had come back

to take Alcmène from her grave and put her on
a bier in the library. He himself was following
on the messenger's heels. Now he was here, and
here lay Alcmène, under the glass globe.

But on all the high-roads of Europe, this
summer night, the couriers of the powers
dashed hither and yon, with every possible political combination in their pockets. All the
chancelleries were still alight, and on all their
country estates the crowned heads of Europe
sat and waited. Joseph in Laxenburg, Charles
at the Escorial, Catherine at Tsarskoe Selo,
George at Windsor — and even the Pope.

219

8

It was not simply that the King had lost a dog, that might be replaced.

All old people grow lonely; their associates are no longer of their own generation. The companions of their youth and their maturity are gone, they speak a language without an echo. The last years had made a fearful void about the King, there was no one left. D'Argens, Seydlitz, Fouqué, Buddenbrock, all gone, Krusemarck and Quintus Icilius within three days of each other; and then the last and the best, the faithfullest of the faithful, the wisest, finest, most upright of all, Earl Marischal Keith. He was all alone. He still had guests at his heavy, unhealthy dinners, but they were nothing to him, they merely gave him his cues for the stories and anecdotes he liked to tell at table. All his mature years he had not known the love of women — and for that there were dark and weighty reasons. In a poor little castle north of Berlin lived the old dame who had been

his wedded wife for fifty years, and once a year
he paid her a half-hour's visit, for very shame.
Once he had had a family, ten brothers and sisters, if he counted right, and four of them must
still be alive. Of them all he had loved only the
clever sister in Bayreuth, and she had been dead
a quarter of a century.

He had nothing else that was near and dear
to him, this great and world-renowned man —
nothing but his dogs.

He had always been fond of dumb animals,
and never allowed anyone to strike or even
tease one in his presence. His riding-horses
knew neither whip nor spur, and he fed them

with his finest fruit, convinced that it tasted
as good to them as to him. His apes might behave as they liked in his rooms, he only laughed,
and when one of them died of consumption, he
ruefully returned the other to its warm native
clime. When a Russian general offered him the
dromedary, he had hesitated to accept the gift,
until he had taken advice of a learned member
of his Academy upon whether the animal could
stand the climate of the Mark. But his greatest, his most genuine and passionate affection
belonged to his Italian greyhounds.

The popular mind must always have a tangible explanation of a fact; and it was the current belief that this passion of the King's dated
from the time, in the Seven Years' War, when
his famous bitch had saved his life by her clever-
ness. The story went that she had been hidden
with the King under the arch of a bridge, when
a troop of pandours, trampling and yelling,
had thundered over it in hot pursuit. The in-
telligent animal had simply looked up at her
master, and neither stirred nor barked. Well,
that was perhaps only a popular saga, good

for popular consumption. But even the upper classes, even international society, has its mob psychology too; and a different story circulated in the capitals of Europe — as concrete as the other, if not so innocent. In this century of erotic abnormalities it was quite simply assumed that the King had his little she-dogs — for he did give she-dogs the preference — to go to bed with, instead of women. It was a story hard to give the lie to, for his favourite dog did actually sleep every night in his bed.

He cared not a whit what they thought of his likes and dislikes. He despised mankind and its opinions, he despised canting morality to such a degree that such rumours as this rather gratified him than otherwise. Nothing was further from his thoughts than to give up any single habit of his on account of a piece of court gossip!

He continued to keep up his breed of Italian greyhounds at the Jägerhof. There were never less than forty, sometimes seventy or eighty, in the care of several keepers. They rued the day when distemper took a heavier toll of these tiny

creatures than the King thought due to inevitable law. He would often come over from
Sans Souci unannounced to strike terror into
them.

The prettiest and cleverest of the dogs he
would have over to the villa on the hill — he
never kept less than three. They were refused
nothing, the King's indulgence knew no
bounds. They sat on the sofas beside him, they
sprang into his lap as he wrote, and he would
put down his pen rather than push the light
burden away. They might play with what they
liked, they might chew what they liked, no matter how costly. They were always with him.
They climbed into his reclining-chair or lay at
his feet as he sat outside in the sun after the
midday meal. And if a strange form were to
come in sight far down the terraces, they would
begin to bark furiously, and he, the misanthrope, would only praise them. They were
only fetched away when he retired — all except
the favourite, who shared his bed. But directly
he waked in the morning, they all came back.

He gave them the tenderest personal care.

Woe to the servant, even the guest, who trod on one of them by accident! The King would fly into a passion, lift his stick, behave quite like his turbulent father. No consideration of etiquette would stay his tongue from administering a violent scolding. Foreigners might have audience with him on important missions, and arrive in full court dress covered with orders, to be ushered by the chamberlain into a room where the King was sitting on the floor with his hat on, dressed in his old coat, feeding his pets and shoving the tidbits to them with his cane.

He could not live without them. The favourite even accompanied him on his campaigns, and almost to the front of battle. And when the King went into winter quarters, an express messenger was sent to fetch the others—by which token the whole world might know that the campaign was over for the year.

In time of peace he moved each year from Potsdam to Berlin for a few weeks' stay. Punctually on the twenty-second of December he would ride thither early in the morning; but the dogs travelled only when the midday sun shone bright. It was a fantastic procession. In the van rocked the Arabian dromedary, with a green saddle-cloth to which was fastened the chest containing the hundred snuff-boxes. The greyhounds followed in a six-horse carriage, each of them buttoned up in a warm coat and covered with blankets as well. A servant sat in the seat at the back, facing the lively little beasts in the well of the coach, and constantly warning them not to get uncovered. When one jumped off the seat, he would lift her back. "Quiet, Rabbitfoot," he would say, addressing them with formality, as though they were persons of rank; "sit still, Pompon, and keep nice and warm. You must not bark like that, Alcmène." It was in Berlin that his darlings became the King's true pleasure and consolation; for the carnival season was on, when, to his indescribable vexation, he had to give several large dinners, attend the bad opera, and even appear at a ball—at which he cut a grotesque figure.

All this the well-disposed dismissed as the

King's whim—the others called it a perverted instinct. And this it was not—yet more than a whim it was. The older he grew, the more he saw of the meanness and vaunting folly of mankind, the more tenderly he turned toward these dumb creatures and rejoiced in their simplicity.

One could believe them. One could count on them. With them one day was like another, you always knew where you were, you were always good friends. Their faces, their little greyhound-physiognomies, would sometimes wear a drolly supercilious expression, but it meant nothing. Sometimes they shivered, even in the sun, so delicately had nature formed them; but they were lively and well. They lived entirely in the present, thus making palpable to that harassed and heavy-laden heart the solid value of each happy moment. They sprang every morning from their beds in full possession of themselves, ever fresh; as it were, ever young; each day as it came was the only one for them, and each was beautiful. They acted like a cordial to his system, oppressed as it was with

227

cares and plans. He worked harder than anyone else, he worked his aides and servants till
they dropped; and this was his refuge, the presence of these lovely joyous creatures without
duties or obligations; he sought it as his Ely-
sium. They never tired or disturbed him, he
gladly gave them all the attention they asked.
The thing he hated most on earth was pretence
—he could not even pass a crucifix without
blaspheming, to show all men he did not believe
that they believed. He took them all for liars
and hypocrites. Only his dogs were free from
hypocrisy. Their naïve egotism touched and
gratified him—it was nature itself.

The times were probably responsible in the
first instance for his choosing greyhounds
rather than any other breed of dogs. The greyhound was your true and genuine rococo dog,
a dog of fashion. But there were solider reasons why he stuck to them all his life, and never
considered any others.

He loved their grace and refinement, the
charming pure line of their limbs. These dogs
and his taste were as un-German as possible.

They were all that his Prussia and his Mark were not — this hardy, cloudy clime in which he always felt like an exile. The breed was called the Italian greyhound; but it was not only Italy it meant to him, the blithe transparent Florentine air. His Athens too, the free, the art-expressive, and his graceful, elegant Paris, spoke to him in his dogs. This Sans Souci was a cloister, and he was the crotchety old abbot. All it possessed of sensuous refinement and the charm of existence it got from these dainty little creatures. He would watch with endless pleasure while they jumped, or lifted their narrow heads, or stretched out their small aristocratic paws close together along the ground; aware all the time of the contrast he himself afforded, with his seven teeth, his tobacco-stained coat, and his fingers knotty with gout.

Always the King loved one of them the most, always there was a little favourite at this court. But there had never been another so dear to him as Alcmène. It was not alone that he was grown so old, and had less than ever any human being near him to whom his heart might turn. It was also that Alcmène herself was so lovely and so wise.

He had carried her in his own arms from the Jägerhof when she was very young. She scarcely weighed a pound, and it seemed a glorious jest to christen this ravishing unearthly toy with the name of Hercules' mother. Even full grown she weighed no more than four; she

230

was the highest and finest result of many years of breeding, surely she was the daintiest, most bewitching greyhound on the earth. And because she was so small, the King could still carry her about, even though his gout got steadily worse.

Alcmène never left him for an hour. Her place was on a low chair near his own, upon a down cushion that scarcely showed any print of her little form. She ate with him; he would lay her little pieces of meat regardless on the damask cloth to let them cool. She walked up and down with him in the gallery and looked at the new paintings. If the King was grave, she felt it at once, and played all her little tricks, sat up or shammed dead — she knew no others, for the King would not have his dogs learn anything. When he spoke to her, she would put her dear little head on one side and listen. But if he scolded, though ever so gently, she could not bear it, and would lay her paw upon his lips as a plea for him to stop. And when she did this the King could not contain his delight. He would spring up, take Alcmène

231

in his arms and press her stormily to his old blue coat; kiss her with his toothless mouth, long kisses and many; and call her by the sweetest names. Sometimes his tears would fall, for very joy of his old, lonely heart. And when at night they went to bed together, Alcmène lay closer than any of her predecessors, snuggled between his breast and his right arm, like a child by its mother, so that he felt her light breath and her gentle warmth against his shoulder.

And now Alcmène was dead.

9

HE had put down his strong-box and his stick and stood with hanging arms and looked down on his darling as she lay. He did not feel the sharpest stab of pain, as one seldom does when one expects it; and moreover Alcmène was so lovely still, so little changed, she seemed still to breathe, and her skin had a clear, golden light, like champagne.

He looked round, close by stood Alcmène's chair, with her little round cushion. Here she had sat and looked on while he governed his kingdom. She always bore herself quietly and with decorum, though her feet would keep up a slight nervous movement, which had torn the cushion in one place so that the feathers showed. That was hard, to look at the little dead form, and by its side this touching evidence of the life that was no more. But something else lay on the chair, Alcmène's collar, a strip of green leather with a little silver plate. He took it up, and read the inscription: *"On m'appelle Alcmène et je suis au roi."* He put his hand on the inside and thought he still felt the warmth of the little neck. He let the collar fall, and wept.

He stood there bowed above the bell-glass, and it seemed as though every tear his old eyes had left to shed gushed from them all at once. He sobbed, he cried aloud, he rubbed his coarse uniform sleeve over his eyes; his face, which had hardly been properly washed for days, was utterly disfigured. His tears flowed on and on, their violence smarted his eyes, they fell upon the shade and rolled to right and left down its glazed sides.

Then a thought shaped itself to a sentence in his mind, and checked his anguish. He thought, and moved his lips to form the words: "These are the last tears I shall ever shed."

The weeping ceased. He took a turn about the little round room, past the glass cases full of works of wisdom bound in red morocco; beneath the empty gaze of Socrates, Apollo, and Homer looking down from their consoles. Three times he made the round of the little cell, his work-room of half a century.

He paused at one of the high windows that

went down nearly to the floor. It was an east
window. Over there at the edge of the terrace
the figure of Flora lay on its beautiful pedestal
in the moonlight. There he himself soon would
lie, beneath this pedestal was his grave. And
close by, his dogs were buried, Alcmène's predecessors in his love. They lay there in a row,
long since reduced to spirit-fine little skeletons,
and above them were small stone tablets with
their names. But at the end of the row, very
black in the moonlight, was a small rectangular
hole, and that was the grave from which they
had taken Alcmène. *"Ma petite Alcmène,"* he
whispered, in the language of his heart, *"bientôt
je coucherai tout près de toi."*

He stepped back to the little table, laid both
his hands flat against the sides of the glass
shade, and lifted it, not without an effort. He
wanted to feel Alcmène once more, to feel how
light she was; he wanted to stroke and kiss her.
But he started back. That she was still un-
touched was but appearance; for beneath the
silken skin was already decay, and the swift
work of death.

He hurriedly replaced the glass shade. A

235

breath of corruption had greeted him, a taint as though from the thousands of wounds, the thousands of infections he had left behind him on his painful way. Oh, peace in death, oh, nothingness, oh, release from guilt!

Once more Alcmène lay shimmering beneath the crystal dome, as though in sleep. But the King in his haste to replace it had not been careful: her body was not quite enclosed within the oval circumference, one of the little legs stuck out. Tender and thin, a spirit paw, it reached out toward the King; to Frederick it was as though his darling put out a dainty hand to draw him after her into the bliss of nothingness.